THIS BOOK DEALS WITH
SENSITIVE AND POTENTIALLY
UPSETTING TOPICS. TRIGGER
WARNINGS INCLUDING
CHAPTER-BY-CHAPTER
SPOILERS ARE PROVIDED ON
PAGE 133.

D1664179

# THE WRITHING SKIES

WRITTEN AND ILLUSTRATED BY

## BETTY ROCKSTEADY

PMMP

**Perpetual Motion Machine Publishing**
Cibolo, Texas

**The Writhing Skies**
Copyright © Betty Rocksteady 2018

All Rights Reserved

ISBN: 978-1-943720-32-3

The story included in this publication is a work of fiction. Names, characters, places and incidents are products of the author's imagination or are used fictitiously. Any resemblance to actual events or locales or persons living or dead is entirely coincidental.

Without limiting the rights under copyright reserved above, no part of this publication may be reproduced, stored in or introduced into a retrieval system, or transmitted, in any form, or by any means (electronic, mechanical, photocopying, recording, or otherwise), without the prior written permission of both the copyright owner and the above publisher of this book.

www.PerpetualPublishing.com

Cover and interior art by Betty Rocksteady
https://www. bettyrocksteady.com/

# ALSO BY BETTY ROCKSTEADY

*Arachnophile*

*Like Jagged Teeth*

# PRAISE FOR
# THE WRITHING SKIES

"The word I would use to describe *The Writhing Skies* is 'nightmarish.' That seems like a run-of-the-mill description for a horror novel, but I mean it more literally. The way the plot progresses often seems to function on dream logic and the imagery is incredibly surreal. In fact, some of the scenes here remind me of actual nightmares I can recall having. The result is gripping and intense."

—Ben Arzate, *Cultured Vultures*

"From the opening chapter, *The Writhing Skies* will have you scratching at your skin as you turn the pages. This book gets deep under your skin, I was constantly looking for blemishes on my forearms, a slight unexplained movement under my skin, the feeling that something was growing inside of me, desperate to introduce itself to the world. This all could be down to the fact that I was high as a kite on meds for a sinus infection I developed a few days prior, or, it could be down to Betty's excellently vivid descriptions? Who knows? I'll leave it for you to decide."

—Adrian Shotbolt, *The Grim Reader*

"Don't let the cover fool you, this isn't some cartoonish fun horror story. This is a dread inducing punch to the stomach, which leaves you feeling hurt and empty inside. It's weird, it's gross, it's beautiful, and it's everything that's horrible in the world wrapped up in a cute odd Betty Rocksteady bubble."

—Scott Kemper, *Signal Horizon*

"This is the first story I have read by author Betty Rocksteady and it makes me ask, 'Where have you been all my life!' *The Writhing Skies* has everything a horror reader wants. Unparalleled atmosphere, constantly building dread and unease, believable characters and an ending that will kick you in the teeth."

—Jim Coniglio, *One-Legged Reviews*

# CHAPTER 1

**IT WAS GOING** to happen again.

Worse this time.

Electricity raised gooseflesh across Sarah's skin and the taste of salt filled her mouth.

No. No. Not again. Pain twisted deep in her gut. Her hands fluttered through the air. Phosphorescence winked in the shadows, where pale blue silhouettes formed. Fireflies tickled up her thighs. Sarah brushed them away and they scattered, but left sticky warmth behind. She wrapped the blanket tightly around herself, covered her head, closed her eyes.

Please go away please go away please go away.

The bed rumbled and shook.

Please, please, don't wanna go out there. Don't wanna move. Don't wanna look.

Invisible hands pried the blankets away, stroked her toes, made curious little sounds and she didn't want to look, she didn't want to see.

For fuck's sake, not even her own apartment was safe. She couldn't leave. She wouldn't leave.

Anything could happen out there.

The buzzing intensified, filled her ears, her heart. *Rrr? Rrr? Rrr?*

She sat up, peeked between the covers. The air shimmered.

It was getting so much worse.

Footsteps shuffled behind the walls. Barely audible, but there. Oh, definitely there.

She nudged blankets aside, jammed feet in slippers. The walls hummed and light glowed, illuminated the apartment in a sickening strobe.

The hallway stretched ahead. Where did she think she was going? The wall moved beneath her hand, caressed her palm. She wouldn't cry. Behind her, the bedroom filled with light and she wouldn't look at it. She would not look.

Outside, or the living room? Oh god, she hadn't left the apartment in . . . how long? Days, weeks, it all blurred together. The floor churned beneath her feet, murmured comforting nothings. The living room could only be worse, but she wasn't ready to face the outside. She couldn't. She couldn't even *look* out there.

She licked her lips, tasted sand.

The living room was dark, shadows askew. The sofa seemed to hover off the floor.

She could hear them in the kitchen. She couldn't picture them, not quite, her mind would not hold the image for long, but she could hear them, soft grunts that thrummed through her pelvis.

She couldn't stay here any longer. She had to go outside, she *had* to, even with the immeasurable sky bearing down on her. She had to go out there with all that open space, where anything could happen.

She had tried to stay here, but it was getting worse.

It had been safe here. For a while, it had been. But she couldn't hide forever.

She needed help.

# THE WRITHING SKIES

Light leaked into the living room, glowing mud that stretched out into fingers. They wanted to touch her. They wanted to ask her something.

She would never make it to the front door. The living room was a mistake. She tripped over the carpet, and bright waves cascaded towards her, wrapped around her, set her carefully on the floor. Impossible hands stroked her cheeks, nibbled her earlobes, asked their incessant wordless questions. *Rrr? Rrr? Rrr?* Warm wet flooded her ears, bubbled in a way that wasn't quite unpleasant, stroked her thighs, slipped between her legs. Sarah moaned. Not again. No more.

Didn't they have enough?

They scattered with a kick and she was able to crawl toward the window.

The things were in the bathroom too, murmuring to each other. With a creak, a corner of a tattered indigo robe peeked out. Colorful mold blossomed on a single long finger, and she had no more time to pretend there were any decisions left to make. She had to go.

She only had her slippers on and all her things, her purse, her phone were in the bedroom and she didn't want to go outside, so stupid, she didn't think this through, but it wasn't safe here anymore. No going back. She yanked the window open and crawled out.

The vast, empty sky hovered above her, a yawning chasm that she couldn't look at. Too many stars, it made her dizzy. She sank to her knees. The rustling inside her apartment had stopped but she was frozen to the ground, unable to move, unable even to make a sound.

The air was so crisp, alive with the smell of blood and the ocean and something else.

Get up the stairs. Get to her neighbor's. They could help. They had to help.

She pulled herself along the wall, bit by bit. Would anyone hear if she called out? Her throat was too thick to try. Couldn't look up from the ground, she couldn't bear to see all that vast open space around her.

The night held its breath in anticipation. She crawled inch by inch to the door. She knocked weakly, then louder, then frantic, and still no one answered.

She forced herself to lift her head. There were no lights on.

There were no lights on anywhere.

Only the florescent light of the sky.

Sarah curled around her knees and wept. The sobs came in waves, a torrent unleashed the moment she let one stray tear slip out. She was weak and sad and she'd rather be dead. Oh god, why hadn't she died?

The night watched her, impassive.

When she caught her breath and wiped the tears away, time had ticked on but nothing had changed. She pulled herself up, steadied herself against the wall.

The street was a chasm of darkness, leading away from her safe apartment. Silent. No lights. Gratefully, she yanked her eyes back and concentrated on getting to her door.

It had been a long time since she had last been outside, too long, and she didn't want to be out here now. They were gone, weren't they? Everything was quiet. They were gone. It was safe again. She wanted her room, blankets, comfort. Things didn't have to change. Not yet. She wasn't ready for them to change.

The door was locked, of course, and her purse was inside. Her phone. Idiot. What was she doing out here? She was fucking insane. Already the sounds of their movements faded from her ears and it couldn't have been what she thought it was. A fucking nightmare or something and hey, she was crazy, right? What other explanation was there for keeping herself cooped up for so long?

Something must be wrong with her.

It was so hard to think.

Back inside. She had to get back inside. She walked across the path, a tightrope walker, gingerly, carefully, because if she took one wrong step she would be plunged back into the nightmare again.

The window was closed. She had not closed it, she would never have closed it. More tears leaked from her eyes as she pounded her fists against the glass, but these ones did not take her over.

She needed to get to Derek. The hell with embarrassment, she couldn't stay out here. Not with the sky watching her like this.

What time was it? Only the hum and faded glow of the streetlights broke up the black silence of the night. Shadows bled in the bushes and she had to force her eyes away. It didn't matter what time it was. She would pound on the neighbor's door until they answered and she would call Derek and he would come get her and make all this bad shit go away.

She could leave this yard. She could walk next door. Maybe she hadn't done it in god knows how long, but she sure as fuck could do it now, if she had to.

# BETTY ROCKSTEADY

Her feet sank into the mud but she kept her eyes straight ahead, scrabbled up porch steps, pounded fists against the huge oak door in front of her, not caring about being polite anymore, not caring who she woke up. Those few steps had taken an incredible amount of courage and they had to wake up, they had to, but no lights went on and Sarah was alone outside.

Did anyone even live here? She couldn't remember the last time she had seen the neighbors. She couldn't remember the last time she had seen anyone.

Sarah walked back to her doorway and crouched, miserable. The wind cut through her thin t-shirt and she wrapped her arms tight around herself. She would wait 'til dawn. She had to. She could not walk up the street, could not walk the half-dozen fucking blocks to Derek's, not in this oily night.

She was an adult and she couldn't even do that. What the fuck was wrong with her?

The night did not abate. She rubbed her hands through her hair, made matted tangles. Cold shook through her body, seeped its way into her bones, and she absolutely did not look up at the sky.

Every time she closed her eyes she could hear them moving, see their tangled shapes, and her eyes snapped back open and she was so, so tired.

And the night did not abate.

# CHAPTER 2

**HER FINGERS HAD** gone numb and her back ached from sitting crunched up against the wall. Sometimes she would almost drift off to sleep, feel that pleasant sense of shifting thoughts that led into dreams. Sometimes things were not so terrible for a little while, but then she would snap back to reality with a chill and a shiver, and she was still sitting outside and the inky dark still surrounded her, and the sky still yawned open, and sometimes she would pound on the door again and shove her face against the window, and maybe a few tears did escape, but not many. Not as many as could.

And then she would sit again and shiver.

The night would not fucking end.

The sky glowed soft.

Too much time had passed and the sun did not rise and she did not look to the sky to see why. It didn't have answers, not the ones she wanted.

She was freezing.

Her fingers were marginally warmer shoved into her armpits. Curled the rest of herself into the doorway, pressed her face against the door. Eventually the street would wake up. It had to. People lived in those houses behind the shadows of trees. People who had to get up and go to work and they would see her and help her.

# THE WRITHING SKIES

A hum snapped her awake. The hum of the streetlights, but more rhythmic. A sigh. Someone speaking in code.

Something massive moved in the bushes and Sarah held her breath. She had been busy worrying about the sky, about getting back in her apartment, she had not thought about what might be out here with her.

A groan, a twisting, something shedding its skin.

Sarah sprang to her feet, faster than she knew she could move.

Pulsing shadows slithered from beneath the bushes, and they rustled, and the light changed and she had no choice now but to run.

Her heart pounded hard in her ears. Breath would not come. Fucking slippered feet stuck to the ground and everything about her body felt huge and awkward and obvious and she moved so slow, it was like the sidewalk was pulling her down, down, down, and the sound of the rustling got further away but she could not stop. So warm from running but the sweat that poured from her face and armpits was freezing cold.

It took forever, but she cleared the block, left dark silent houses behind, stumbled over the curb, and the rumbling behind her stopped and so did she.

The street yawned ahead and behind her. None of these houses looked familiar. None of them looked right. Grey and featureless in the luminescent blue light of the stars. They did not look like real houses at all, looked more like cardboard cutouts wedged behind bushes.

Sarah didn't know which way to turn.

She did not want to plunge deeper into the city but the comfort of Derek's arms beckoned, the one person who could make everything right, and why the fuck hadn't he called?

Things could still be okay between them, it was just so far. So achingly far away and she was cold and the night was dark, and it felt like eyes were looking at her from every bush, from every tree.

She turned back to look towards her apartment and her head lolled heavy on her neck, everything moved in slow motion.

A tangled figure clad in glinting sapphire darted out of sight behind the building, and bile rose in Sarah's throat.

No choice then.

Forward.

Shaking step by shaking step.

It wasn't right for the street to be this quiet.

Her footsteps were liquid slow, but she kept moving, three blocks, four blocks, five, and finally, Derek's house. Peeling siding, unmown lawn, broken bottles in the gutters, and it had never looked so beautiful. A sob rose in Sarah's throat. She crept carefully past the shadows. Those eyes were still upon her. If she didn't look, if she didn't act scared . . .

Frogs croaked somewhere, and constellations swirled dizzying patterns behind her eyes. Keep moving.

The grass in the yard was grey and dusty, snapping beneath her feet. Her slippers left damp footprints. She crawled up the steps and if the lights were out, it had to be because it was so late. Derek was home. He had to be home. Fuck, even if he wasn't, his dad must be. His dad *never* left the house, was always folded up on the couch, drinking cheap beer and belching and screaming profanities at Derek or his sister every time they so much as moved.

# THE WRITHING SKIES

Sarah approached the door, pounded, waited, closed her eyes and listened for the footsteps that were surely coming. She knocked again, again, and the tears were coming and she couldn't stop them now, where the fuck was Derek? Where could he possibly be?

Sarah tore her eyes away from the door.

Not a light on anywhere. Rustling movement in backyards. Nothing else.

"Hey!" Fuck her if she got the wrong attention, but her voice ripped out of her throat and she couldn't stop it. "Derek, it's me, it's me, it's me, please, please, please." She begged the door, and nothing, and nothing.

Her voice echoed down the street.

The bushes went quiet.

Sarah's heart pounded into her throat. Her words were the only sound in all this quiet grey muck and she could feel the attention of the night turn towards her, she could feel that she had interrupted something very quiet and very still.

The top of the hill, a blur of movement, something glowing and twisting.

She had to get out of here.

The shed. The flashlight. Better than nothing.

The yard was darker than she could ever remember it being—when had they gotten so many trees? Their shapes were changed, taller and hulking with gnarled roots. A thin grey gravy squirted up from the grass, covered her slippers, but she trudged through and darted around the back, pressed herself against the wall. Caught her breath.

Nothing had seen her.

Had it?

## BETTY ROCKSTEADY

The shed leaned heavy to one side. There was an old mattress in there, one she knew all too well, but she would be behind four walls, she could wait out the night, hidden. She wrenched on the door and a fat azure spider—*it had to be a spider it must be a spider what else could it be*—darted out of the keyhole, danced across her hands, almost made her scream again, almost felt like it crawled down her throat and would scatter its webs and make a new home there.

The door wouldn't open.

There was no way in.

Across the street, a curious buzzing.

# CHAPTER 3

**P**EOPLE IN TATTERED coats approached. Sarah couldn't bear to look at them. Milky, dirty skin, covered in scraps of glowing sapphire that undulated like jellyfish. They lit up everything, their soft light spread towards her and Sarah had to go, had to go, had to run, had to hide.

The disgusting grass stole her slippers, sucked them up, and her bare feet splattered against soft slug bodies, and she held her breath while she ran and plunged into the bushes that separated Derek's yard from the neighbor's.

Tiny branches scratched across her cheeks and she would not make a sound, she curled up, made herself as small as she could, let the bushes cover her, let herself become the bushes, and she held her head in her hands and waited.

She squinted against the glow.

If she did not look, if she did not see, maybe they would leave her alone.

*Rrr?*

Bushes rustled around her and she clenched her eyes shut so tight, she grit her teeth, and the branches scratched her arms and something soft and slick wound against her feet. Her mouth opened to scream but the spider in her throat scrabbled and nothing came out.

Something, a tentacle, a snake, rubbed between her toes, caressed her feet and she opened her eyes but the light was too bright and she closed them again.

*I'm okay I'm okay I'm okay it's okay it's okay it's okay.*

A raspy tongue wound between her toes, trailed a sweet-smelling lubrication. The thing in her throat moved, burst, excreted a thick nectar. It tasted sweet and metallic. Intoxicating. Sarah's mouth hung open, dainty legs clawed their way out, left a trail of drool.

Softness trailed from her toes, tickled the soles of her feet. Whisper soft, it slid beneath the folds of fabric at her ankle, wrapped around her calf.

It pressed against her, a cat's tongue, slimier, stickier. The sensation trailed her knee, up her thigh, smooth and wet. Everywhere it touched flooded with warmth. Her mouth filled with honey.

So many hands, everywhere, not hands, tongues and shapes and she couldn't open her eyes, couldn't close her mouth. Her cunt yawned open, blossomed and made its own sweet wet juices in response to the touch.

Delicate tingling threads tickled her wrists, her feet, and those appendages went numb, heavy, dead. No pain. No pain. Relax. Relax.

*I'm okay I'm okay I'm okay.*

Jelly slid up her thighs, coated them hot and slick, pressed against her snatch. Then she couldn't help herself, she pressed back against it, and it vibrated and hummed and throbbed. Tingling goop soaked her panties, leaked inside, made her moan. Slick and soft, it dribbled inside her, and she arched her back and it hardened in response, filling her almost too full, too hard, too hard, stretching her painfully, then soft again, flexing against the throbbing walls of her insides.

More fingers slithered beneath her waistband, tiny soft tongues that slithered and sucked her labia, thrummed against her clit, and the gel inside went soft and hard and poured out of her and slid back in and she writhed and tried to open her mouth to scream or moan or do something, anything.

*Rrr? Rrr? Rrr?* something was calling and it was hard to breathe around the legs that tickled in her throat, it was hard to think anything at all, the thing hardened and softened and expanded inside her, too big, then too small, leaving her aching and empty and she bucked against it, pressure building building building begging to be released.

And more fingers snaked up against her smooth belly, cradled it in sticky tingling hands. It moved, it moved in a way she had never felt before, like her skin turned inside out, gripped between strong thick hands and flipped, the tender inside of her muscles screaming, and *agony agony agony* her skin ripped and tore and something sprayed across her belly, and her skin peeled away and she tasted acid in the back of her throat as her skin bubbled and one final caress, one final sting, and it slithered away.

Finally her limbs were free but they were dead and aching and she couldn't scream, could only gasp for breath. Her pussy ached, felt stretched out, too empty, and her guts sang in pain. Her hands and feet were numb and useless, but slowly her arms and legs moved and they started to tingle back to life.

A familiar pattern of light blinked across her eyelids. Her eyes were sticky and opened reluctantly.

# THE WRITHING SKIES

The bushes filtered out the light and covered her in comforting darkness. Everything was quiet.

The pain faded, but her stomach 'was changed. Her hand fluttered. She didn't want to touch it but she couldn't help herself. Her fingers came away slimy, tacked together. She held them close to her face to see—blood, pus, what? And they shone with a mucusy phosphoresce and she buried them in the dirt, frantically scrubbing them clean, leaving muddy spots behind.

Her cunt was soaked, and she wanted to wipe that off too, but she had nothing, so she just rubbed her hand into her crotch, and a gush of something emptied into her underwear and it felt clammy and awful but she couldn't do anything about that now. She had to go.

The branches shifted around her. They were mean, they scratched her with sticks and thorns and dug open rivulets on her arms but she kept crawling.

She kept crawling.

The bushes were too deep, she should have been out by now but they just kept fucking going. She tunneled forward, and the quality of light didn't change, and it was like she was scrabbling in place, because the brambles stayed thick and impenetrable and she should have been in the next yard by now, should have been there long ago.

Nicks and scratches sang. Long fingers caressed her shoulders as she passed, and the pain in her gut faded and she kept crawling and kept crawling and maybe she would be tunneling forward like this forever but finally she pulled herself out of the bushes and fell into the neighbor's yard, grey and blank.

A swing set wobbled in the dim light, leftovers

from someone else's childhood. 'She wobbled when she stood up, made her way over to it. Her shirt was scratched and torn, and something peeked out from a tear across her stomach out and she wasn't ready to look at it, not yet. She needed a minute. She needed. Please, just . . . something.

The swing was damp but held her weight. She sank gratefully into it. She should still be running, shouldn't she, but where would she run to? The windows were dark, and if she thought she could see someone peeking out, someone pale and long, surely it was her imagination and they weren't moving and she just didn't want to look. She was tired. Why wasn't she still in bed? Why wasn't she somewhere safe?

Her mother's house was more long streets away, but where else could she go? Tiffany's place was even further, and she couldn't fucking drag Tiffany into her shit again. No, back to Mom's. Crawling back, like Mom always said she would. Derek wasn't there for her, and she had nowhere else to turn.

The night was absolutely silent. Even the swing set didn't squeak.

Sarah looked at her feet, bare and filthy, because she couldn't bear to look at anything else. Not her stomach, not the face in the window, and not the awful sky that squirmed above. She should have stayed in her room. The panic hadn't abated, but it was tired now. It didn't make her feel like running anymore. She wanted to cry, but the tears didn't come.

Her hand made its way towards her belly again, but she chased it away. Insistent, it slid back, rested against the soft stained material of her t-shirt, and something shifted.

# THE WRITHING SKIES

Her feet moved of their own volition, and the ground was gritty beneath them, and she started walking.

# CHAPTER 4

**THE ROADS WERE** longer than she remembered, the streetlights a pustular shade of green that faded quickly into shadow.

Things moved in the bushes. Watched from windows. Hovered at the tops of the streets and she didn't look, she wouldn't look, she made up for the fear by just moving moving moving.

Maybe it wasn't fair, but it felt like this was on purpose. Like he had let her down again.

Her chest ached and she had to keep blinking back tears. Why hadn't she gone to Mom in the first place? God, what was wrong with her that she wasn't worried about her family in all this? The people who were really important?

Where the fuck was Derek when she needed him, ever?

Things slithered in back yards and she could feel their eyes on her. Her thighs stuck together and her stomach itched and she jammed her hands tightly under her armpits, so she wouldn't scratch it. The tingling was maddening. 'Not painful, not exactly, but it felt different than the skin around it. She could feel the outline blur and spread, something that dripped and grew, and she didn't want to think anymore. Just watch her feet walk on the concrete. Don't think. Keep moving.

# BETTY ROCKSTEADY

The shortest way to Mom's was past the adult school. Everyone ended up there a couple years after dropping out, and she had been no different. Derek had taken a few years longer to make his way back. There was a huge tree that she and Derek and Tiffany used to sit under at lunch break. Maybe she could rest there for a few minutes. The lights were giving her a headache and she wanted to close her eyes. Put her back to the tree, and the fence would protect her from the side, and she would see anything that was coming. She would be hidden.

No. She had to keep going.

The street that led down to the school was bathed in shadow. Cold leeched from the sidewalk up into her bare feet. They ached already. She didn't spend much time outside, her feet were used to comfortable carpet and slippers, and this abuse scratched and tore them.

The street was *so* dark. If something were in the shadows between the houses, she would never see it until it was too late. Maybe she just hadn't knocked hard enough at Derek's, maybe . . .

When she looked back, there were two of them. Their bodies shifted and moved beneath their cloaks, and the cloaks themselves seemed to change and writhe. They squirmed over the bodies beneath, and before they could turn and see her, Sarah darted down the street, to the school.

She skirted the fence and approached the front path. The building came into sight and Sarah's throat went dry. The grounds were bare, but the lights were on. A pale glow leaked out the windows, illuminated the parking lot, not quite touching the yard.

It was the first normal light she had seen since leaving her apartment, the first light not connected to those things. She hesitated at the periphery of the school, watched the windows.

Who could be in there? There could hardly be classes this late. Other people like her? Stuck in these dark streets and finally finding a place to be safe. Or . . .

A branch cracking in the distance sounded like a gunshot. Sarah whirled and the figures were closer, not yet looking her way, but the way they moved, the way they *rippled*, set off a rapid fire in Sarah's heart and she suddenly realized how exposed she was, standing here, gaping at the school.

She couldn't go in there. Not yet. She needed to watch for a little longer, figure out what was going on. And what about her mom? Get to the tree. Hide out. Figure out what to do next. Just a few minutes, just to catch her breath and build up her nerve.

If she went up front where the gate opened she would be right in the light and anyone looking out the windows would see her. The wire fence in front of her was a better bet. Sarah had never been the most athletic, but it was only up to her neck, and she was sure she could scale it.

The metal was cold beneath her feet. She hoisted herself up, swung a leg over top, trying to be so quick and quiet. Her t-shirt caught and tore and she couldn't help but let out a little gasp as the wire brushed against her belly, right where the thing had touched. Her ass smacked against the ground. Stars danced in front of her eyes, and she tried not to look at the hunk of glowing mold she left on the fence. She crawled on hands and knees across the yard. To the tree.

It was reassuring to see it there, stretching above her, branches to the sky. It was one of the few things that looked right this evening. It looked like it belonged here, it looked like she remembered, deep browns and vivid greens, not yet changed into grey shadows by this endless fucking night.

She ducked behind it to hide from the lights and in the shadows, something moved, and she nearly screamed.

"Sarah?"

# CHAPTER 5

**SHE COULDN'T CALM DOWN**. Her breathing would not normalize, no matter how hard she tried, and the tears were agonising, embarrassing in their intensity.

"Sarah, it's okay, it's me." Derek grabbed her wrist, pulled her closer. They curled under the tree and she got her first good look at him in . . . weeks? Months? How long had she been cooped up in that apartment?

He didn't look well. The crisp lines of his cheekbones were hollowed out, haunted looking. His eyes danced wild in their sockets, he couldn't stop looking around, could barely look at her.

"What? What?" Her mouth was thick around words that she couldn't quite get out. "What are you doing here?"

"Shhh, shhh, it's okay." The embrace he pulled her into was warm and he smelled sweaty and scared and oh fuck, the tears again.

"Derek, what the fuck is going on out here? How did you get here? What are you doing?" The words were a jumbled mess. She couldn't even hear what she was saying, it was just a drone in her ears. The smile that twitched at his lips made something move in her stomach.

"I have no idea what's going on. I'm in the same boat as you." There was no fear in his face, but the wild look was still in his eyes. Was he on something? Or was he just . . . scared? She hadn't seen him scared before. Well, not this kind of scared. A different kind.

She didn't want to say it. "I was at your house. I was looking for you. Your phone! Do you have your phone? Mine . . . I left mine inside. We need to call someone. My mom. Do you think she's okay? Have you seen anyone?"

He shook his head. "I've been sitting out here for ages, trying to decide. Do you think we should go in there?" Something buzzed by his ear, flitted away.

"What, in the school? Are you nuts? There's something in there. I'm not . . . I don't think it's safe. Do you think it's safe? Do you think it has to do with—"

"We're not safe out here. I don't like it outside. The sky . . . "

"I haven't been outside much. At all. Fuck. I'm so confused. What is happening here? You could have come to see me.""

"I haven't been much of anywhere lately, Sarah." She looked at him again. His right hand was shoved in his pocket. On his left hand, his nails and cuticles were all chewed up. Maybe she hadn't been the only one hiding out in her apartment. Had he been holed up in his parents' basement all this time?

"I need to call my mom. Do you have your phone?"

Half a smile appeared on Derek's face. "What do you think she's gonna do?"

"I just . . . do you have it?"

Derek pulled his hand out of his pocket. "Yeah, I don't know why I kept it though. The fucking thing doesn't work." He handed her the phone and she tried to turn it on. It was too warm. 'Soft as clay. The buttons indented with her fingerprints and the screen pulsed with a head splitting green.

"Piece of junk." Derek snatched it back from her and threw it. It disappeared silently into the grass.

"I—"

He clamped his hand over her mouth. Asshole. "Shut up, I hear something."

A sick mix of feelings churned inside her, feelings she couldn't pin down. Anger, yeah, but beneath that, sadness, and something else, something worse. After a moment, he released her. That look was back in his eyes. "Have you seen them?"

"Yeah. The . . . the people, you mean?" The pale faces. The changing sky. The long fingers. The way they looked at her. The way they touched her.

"Yeah. I don't want to run into them. I can't take it." He took her hand in his, awkwardly, but their fingers fit together so naturally. A familiar thing to look at, but it was all wrong now, wasn't it? When was the last time he had been nice to her, made her feel good? Oh, it didn't matter.

"What should we do?" Fuck, she just could not stop the tears from coming, and then he was pulling her close, kissing them away, and he wrapped his arm around her shoulders and she felt so much better, so much better just for a few seconds and it ached, oh it ached so much, it ached in her gut and in her head and in her heart. He pulled away and shoved his hands back in his pockets, embarrassed. She leaned her head on his shoulder.

"I don't want to go in there."

"Okay. We don't have to." And he just held her.

# THE WRITHING SKIES

They didn't talk for a while. She kept her eyes low. She didn't want to look at the creatures buzzing around them. She was so scared, but she didn't want to tell him, didn't want to state the obvious. She was still afraid of saying the wrong thing, so she just looked at his face, waiting for clues about how he felt or what she should do. His jaw twitched, his hand clenched and unclenched. His skin looked bad, and stubble ticked across his normally clean shaven face. He could always handle everything but now . . .

It was far too cold for a summer night. Sarah curled her feet under herself, wrapped her arms around her churning stomach. The silence stretched on, grew awkward. Shouldn't they be talking? Was he waiting for her to say something? He was so close beside her, but he was miles away. He still wouldn't look at her. "It's so cold out here."

Derek didn't reply. He looked into the distance, at the grey mist that swirled through the streets. Her chest ached. Shouldn't they be doing something? Shouldn't something have happened by now? She pushed in closer to Derek, and he didn't respond.

"I missed you." The words sounded so stupid coming out of her mouth.

"I still think we should see what's going on in there. I don't like sitting out here. I feel like we're just waiting for something to happen."

Did he think *she* liked it? "Do you really think it's safe? I'd rather . . . I want to check on Mom. What about your dad? Is he okay?"

He sighed, exacerbated. "You really want to go to your mom's? She fucking hates me. I doubt she'll be too happy to see me in the middle of all this. The school is right here and there's people in it."

She wouldn't cry. "I don't wanna split up. Not now. But I have to make sure she's okay. Please? We can use her phone. It's only a couple blocks. Please." The school didn't look right. It didn't feel right, not at all.

"Sarah . . . I don't think anyone's okay." He sighed. "Fine. We'll do what you want to do. Let's get this over with."

# CHAPTER 6

**I**T WAS AWKWARD now between them, but it would get better. It *had to* get better, once they were safe somewhere. Inside. Once she knew Mom was safe. Not out here under the twisted sky. Derek held her hand as they walked, but they didn't speak, and that was for the best, wasn't it, because what would they possibly say?

She could have made the walk herself, and maybe she should have. Derek seemed annoyed, and there was no way to pacify him, not if they wanted to hurry, and stay quiet, and stay out of sight.

Milky orbs bobbled around them, leaking cold light. Derek hunched his shoulders, wouldn't look at her. It wasn't safe out here.

"I don't know what you think your mom is gonna do."

She wished he would be quiet. The orbs whirred, spun, doubled back, making her dizzy. "I just wanna make sure she's okay." Now that they were nearly there, she didn't know what she was thinking either. She was tired. The lights made her head ache.

"Everything's dark. Where the fuck is everybody?"

He was right. The greenish light let them see where they were going, but none of the houses had so much as a porch light on. "It's late . . . "

"Something is really wrong here. We should have gone in the school."

Sarah shrugged. Too late. They were here now. Her mother's house had never looked so foreign. Cold. The color of the siding looked slightly off, but that had to be just the lighting.

Sarah pressed her face against the door. The glass was cold. She wanted to close her eyes. She wanted to be inside, but now that she was here, she was afraid to knock. Afraid to know for sure. The dread that circled her stomach turned to lead and she felt full and sick and this had been a mistake.

"Tell me you at least have a key."

"No."

He made an irritated sound. Her knock was like a thunderclap, too loud. Heat flooded her cheeks and she glanced back. Pale green buzzed from the end of the street, nothing else.

"She's not fucking home. No one is home. We should have went in the school. I knew we should have."

"What makes you think that was any safer? God, you didn't have to come."

"You didn't give me much choice. What was I gonna do, send you off into the night all alone?"

Her stomach twisted again. No hope. Nothing. She knocked again.

"Something's coming."

Yeah, she heard it too.

*Rrr?*

"I don't wanna be out here." Derek's voice rose an octave. "I don't wanna be out here when they get here. Can we break a window or something? Let's get inside. I wanna be inside."

"Break a window?" Her voice warped and slowed as tiny bursts of light exploded in her vision. Was that her eyes, or more of the fireflies? Waving her hand in front of her face didn't help; it was the fireflies, and they clung to her fingertips, tingling.

Derek grabbed her, pulled her around the side of the house, and her mom was there, she was standing in the window, thank fucking god, Mom was there, she was fine, she would let them in.

*RrrrRrr?*

Light glinted off the window.

'Mom's eyes were flat and dark.

"Sarah . . . "

"Mom!" The window curved beneath her fists, pliant. Mom didn't budge. Her face didn't so much as flicker.

"Sarah, something's not right here." More lights buzzed. Everything tingled. Her throat was thick with honey, with something that tasted so good but so strange. Mom wasn't moving, but that was okay.

Mom's skin fluttered. It was sallow, almost green. Dull. Derek pulled her to the side, pointed.

Everything inside the house was wrong, all wrong. Cardboard cutouts. The couch wasn't there. The window wasn't a window. It was a membrane. Something was buzzing. Mom fell apart, a pile of scraps, a buzzing mound of glowing flesh and the door creaked open and light burst out and all the doors on the street burst open and the light was blinding and it was in her eyes and her nose and her mouth and honey slipped down her throat and she could barely keep her eyes open all of a sudden, it was all too much, she was exhausted, she was falling.

Derek moaned. Sarah's head swiveled toward

him. She stumbled, shook her head, tried to blink the light away. Derek was on his knees, luminescent, mouth open and glowing. "Derek!" Her voice was so far away, then bright hot pain as she slapped herself across the face.

Whispers and bright flashing lights and squishing bodies clustered all over Derek, slithering, humming. "Get off him!" She waved her hands and the little fluttering orbs scattered. Derek's eyes were far away.

"What did you do that for? They felt nice."

"I'm sorry.' Something's wrong here. We shouldn't be here." She pulled him up, dragged him behind her, his hand in hers, as it should be. Her throat was still sticky and full with sweetness'. Her eyes blurred and ached and she wished she could close them, just for a few minutes. The sky flashed. Distantly, she thought she could hear laughing but that was impossible' and oh god, this was all her fault.

"I'm sorry," They were back at the school, the streets had folded under their feet and somehow they were here and collapsing under the tree and Derek had been right and she was so sorry.

"I told you. I told you."

"What happened to my mom? Where is everyone? What's happening?" Where had they been? Her mind wouldn't hold on to it. Images flickered through her mind, but they felt like a dream. Had they left this spot at all? Had they been here the whole time?

Derek wouldn't look at her. Was he crying? He couldn't be crying.

"I don't know. Shut up. We should have gone in the school."

Her head hurt so bad. "I know. I'm sorry. I really am." Everything was spinning.

"We'll go in there and people will be there and they'll help us. Like we should have done in the first place." Derek stood up, wobbled.

"Wait." She wasn't ready. She wasn't ready to move at all. She couldn't. While she was here, with him, under the tree, she could pretend things were normal. Closer to normal. She couldn't look at the things out there anymore. Everything hurt and she was so scared. "Can't we just stay here? Just for a little while?"

Derek sank to his knees. "Yeah. In the morning. We'll go in the morning." He wrapped his arms around his head and curled against the tree.

# CHAPTER 7

**I**T WAS IMPOSSIBLE to sleep. Ridiculous to even try stretched out on the frozen ground. Her feet were icy sore. The tree shaded them from anything that might be out there, but she kept hearing things. Even the slightest sound made her jump. Derek curled against her back. His body was cold too. There was no way to get comfortable. Her side ached, she wanted to roll over, but she didn't want to move and irritate him. His arm felt good around her and she didn't want him to turn away.

His breathing was slow, steady.

How could he sleep at a time like this?

Her eyes tried to flicker to the sky but she brought them back.

Eventually, she drifted.

The cold stayed with her, got deep into her bones. She tried to ignore it, just listen to Derek's breathing, concentrate on how it made her feel. Forget what was going on out there. She'd go crazy if she kept thinking about it. This had once been her favorite thing to do, lie beside Derek and be held and just . . . just feel how love made her feel. Let herself be sucked into his embrace. Maybe she could pretend they were somewhere else, wound tight together on the sofa in his room, napping together on a long Sunday afternoon, tired out from drinking the night before.

The air was so wet and cold. It ruined the illusion. Her chest clenched and she coughed, couldn't help it. Derek sighed beside her. She had ruined the moment, but he pulled her closer, tighter, and she tried to relax.

He pressed his pelvis against her ass, but he was probably just asleep. There was a faint buzz in her ears and that strange taste flooded her mouth again. She pulled away, slightly. It wasn't a good time for that, not now, not in the middle of all this. Derek moved closer again.

His cock hardened as he pressed rhythmically against her. Sarah tried to slow her breathing, pretend she was asleep. Leave me alone. Please, just leave it.

But his hand was against her ass, rubbing, squeezing. He whispered into her ear, "I missed you. Can you feel how much I missed you?"

"I miss you, Derek. I do, but right now?"

"Come on. I know all this sucks. I want to feel better. It's okay. Let me make you feel better too." Hot breath on her neck. His hand slipped down her pajamas pants.

*"Come on, it's okay." His cock was in her hand and she was wet and everything was slippery and happening so fast. It was okay, wasn't it? Not her first, but their first time together, and they were in love, or she was at least, and he couldn't be far behind. Four months was a long time to be dating and he had been in her hand and in her mouth and he was all wrapped up in her heart and she wanted to, she did, but right now?*

*No one would disturb them, no one knew they were here. Derek's dad was inside watching TV, but* he hadn't seen them sneak back to the shed, didn't know they were skipping class. They were alone, yeah, but it was cold and dirty and she would rather be in her own bed, taking their time, not like this, but he pressed against her and kissed her ear. "Come on, I want you so bad, so bad, you're so hot, come on, Sarah, it's okay." He slid a finger inside her and she gasped. "You're so fucking wet, I know you want it too. Come on. It'll feel so good."

"Do you have a condom?" Just like that, the decision was made and her chest felt so hot and her cheeks flushed and this was it, they were going to do it.

"No, don't worry, it's fine, I won't come inside you."

Shit. This was happening way too fast. She had wanted to wait until their six-month anniversary, they had both said that was when they would do it, but he was rolling her onto her back. He kissed her neck, slid his hands up beneath her shirt, pressed his cock against her belly. His tongue slid down her neck, sucked her nipple into his mouth and teased it with his teeth. Fingers teased her hole, then slammed inside her, pressing against her G-spot. Lips on her stomach, then on her slit, and wetness poured out of her to meet his mouth. He moved back up and kissed her, and she tasted herself. Hands slid beneath her ass, pushed her legs up towards her head.

"No wait, stop, wait a minute."

He rubbed the head of his cock against her. "It'll be okay." Then he drove himself in up to the hilt and it was so much bigger than his fingers and she groaned and it was too late.

"Oh god, you're so tight, oh fuck."

*"Derek, slow down, it hurts, slow down." But he didn't slow down, he went faster and she didn't want to yell too loud, she didn't want anyone to hear. His cock felt huge, felt bigger than it had ever felt in her hand, felt like it was tearing her. "Please, please."*

*"Uhghh." He tilted her hips up further, squeezed her ass, kneaded it, kept slamming his dick into her, pummelled her with it, and oh god, someone was going to hear.*

*"Derek," she hissed, but he kept going and slammed into her with such force her head hit the wall.*

*"Oh shit." He yanked his dick out and it was already spurting and her face was wet and she didn't want him to see.*

He was pulling her pants down. It was so fucking cold. It was too cold for this. But she didn't want to get in a fight, didn't want to be alone out here in all this. Not now. He wrapped his hand around the back of her head, kissed her cheek. The dirt felt itchy against her ass. She wiggled away, but only a little.

"Hey, hey, it's okay. Let's just . . . let's just feel better. Please baby, help me feel better. I missed you so much." Everything in her body was tense. She glanced up at the sky, glanced back into his eyes. They were familiar, at least. He was scared too, and seeing that made her feel a little sorry for him.

"I'm not comfortable," she murmured, but she could feel herself giving in. One hand nestled between her thighs, the other slid up beneath her shirt, and her skin moved in response.

"Oh god, what the fuck is this?" His voice was too loud.

"What?" She shifted away from him, pulled her pants back up.

"Sarah what the fuck is this?" His right hand was covered in . . . something. Wet and slick and shining. It looked like phlegm, like something coughed up from deep inside you that wasn't supposed to come out. "It's all over you! Why didn't you say something?"

She peeled her shirt away from her stomach. A snot-like sheen glazed her, released a sweet rotten scent. Knots of green and yellow twisted around her belly, kissed her belly button.

"Oh no." Bile rose in her throat. "No, no, nope." She yanked her shirt down, used the cloth to wipe herself off. Wet chunks dribbled, sank into the ground, but beneath what she wiped away there was more and it got on her hands and it tingled and stung and felt horrible and the more she wiped, it just kept blossoming, it just kept coming, and it started to hurt, the bits that ripped off pulled deeper things out and she couldn't do it anymore and she was panicking, and Derek was looking at her in disgust.

He wiped his hands on his pants, skin shining with residue. "This fucking hurts, what are you, diseased or something? How could you let me touch this? Fuck, Sarah! You should have said something."

"Oh god, what's wrong with me?"

"Well whatever it is, it's wrong with the both of us now. For fuck's sake."

"Do you think it's okay? What do you think it is?" She couldn't keep her hands off it. More sloughed away, and where was her skin? She should be into her skin now, the gunk shouldn't go this deep. How deep did it go? How deep did it fucking go?

"Shut up," Derek hissed, and she couldn't stop the tears streaming down her face and she couldn't stop looking into the crater in her gut, but Derek yanked on her arm and pointed, and he didn't need to point because she could see the glow but she couldn't stop looking at her stomach and the shapes that curled and twisted there.

They were coming down the street, too many of them, illuminating the night, a slow steady progression of glowing figures.

"For Christ's sake, stop crying." He yanked her shirt back down over her stomach, then glanced at his hand. His face twisted in disgust. He shoved it into his pocket, but not before Sarah caught a glimpse. She wished she hadn't. Was that her fault? It looked worse than it should have, quicker than seemed possible. Diseased, rotten, leaking thick phlegm. "Just stop crying for one fucking second."

Telling her to stop crying made it worse. She wiped her hand across her face. Everything was sticky and awful and horrible and *what was wrong with her stomach?*

"We can't stay out here, okay? This is stupid. We have to do something. I'm sick of sitting around waiting for it to get worse. Waiting for those fucking things to find us."

Her face felt sore and swollen. She looked horrible when she cried. Derek wouldn't look at her. "What do you want to do?" She didn't want him to be mad at her. Yeah, maybe he *was* a shit, but they only had each other right now.

"I want to see what's going on in the school, like I said in the first place. We might be able to get help there." His brow furrowed. She could see where wrinkles would appear in just a few years. "Are you coming or not? You can wait here if you really want to, climb up in the tree or something. I'm going now.

I'm not gonna stand around here any fucking longer."

She peeked between the branches again. The creatures didn't seem to be getting any closer. They didn't seem as *there* anymore. Pale, wispy forms, foggy green. Their robes looked indistinct, tatters that waved and teased the pavement.

What were they doing? What were they waiting for?

"I just don't think it's a good idea. Can't we wait—?"

But Derek snorted and walked away. He turned his back to her, and was she really surprised? A throb of hate wound its way up her throat, made her nauseous with the desire to prove him wrong, to show him that she could be brave.

It didn't matter. She didn't want him to get further away. She couldn't stay out here on her own.

They had to stick together, whether he liked it or not.

She followed.

# CHAPTER 8

**D**EREK HEADED STRAIGHT for one of the side doors. He didn't slow down, didn't even look back to see if she was coming.

"Hey,"she mumbled. He barely glanced back when she touched his shoulder. "I'm sorry." What was she apologising for? Fuck. It didn't matter.

The windows were blurry and glowing. Couldn't he see how wrong this was? But if he did, he didn't care. He had made up his mind, and when Derek made up his mind there was no talking around it.

Things moved in the light, things that were made of light too. People? God, let it be people like them, even if they had no idea what was going on either, just having more people to be around would be such a fucking relief. She wouldn't have to count on Derek. As if she could.

Derek yanked the door open and slid inside, leaving her to catch it before it slammed shut. The light glaring from the window made her guts crawl. Her stomach rippled and cramped, pain quaked through her body and it was not a good idea to go inside, there was something wrong inside, but just as she started to turn away, the lights changed, and the sky *screamed,* then the sound of massive teeth grinding and she couldn't look she couldn't stay out here and so she followed Derek inside.

The lurid green burned her retinas, and behind the screaming light, bright dots flashed, colorful, wriggling, dancing and exploding and changing. Derek groaned somewhere nearby and she reached for him, grabbed the back of his shirt, and he moved away. She rubbed her eyes and the glare faded.

The hallway was longer than she remembered.' The lockers that lined the walls were shiny, metallic. They must have been replaced. They were too new to belong here. Derek stood in the center of the hallway in front of her, looking dazed. He wobbled slightly on his feet and stumbled toward a branching corridor. Sick yellow light spilled onto his profile, and in that light his face looked blank, featureless.

A chattering echoed from the hall.

"What do you see?" That whimper didn't sound like her, the way it squeaked in her throat and died.

He glanced back, his eyes empty orbs sunk deep in his face. His skull glowed beneath paper-thin skin. "I'm late for class, I'll catch you later!" His feet seemed to glide across the floor, and he disappeared down the corridor.

"Derek!" She should have been terrified, but she went after him. A rope that led from her heart to him tugged her along. The new corridor was pale and hazy, and all the doors were closed. No sign of him. "Derek!" She stepped into the hall, and the air wriggled around her. She peered inside the first door—he couldn't have gone far—and she was pounding on it and screaming and light flashed inside. Figures moved but she couldn't tell what they were doing. They didn't move right, flowing and pouring and bending at impossible angles. She watched them and tasted blood.

The chattering didn't stop. The doorknob spun uselessly in her hands. She backed away, so light, so dizzy, the air so strange, too hard to breathe. She had to get out of here. No, she had to find Derek. Branches of hallway gaped around her, leading to more gleaming lockers. The light that glinted off them splintered into her brain and she winced at the sudden shock of the headache.

Which way had she come in? Everything looked the same. Where the fuck had Derek gone? Lips pressed together, she firmed her jaw against tears. She didn't want to cry but she couldn't fucking take this one minute longer.

She was alone again.

All the classroom doors opened at once.

*Rrr? Rrr? Rrr?*

A murmur of too many voices that licked their way inside her ears without making an ounce of sense.

Sarah stepped back, away from the memory of that writhing sky, those strange lights . . .

It didn't matter. There wasn't time. They came streaming out of the classrooms. Those tattered robes weren't robes at all, they were fluttering panels of flesh in sallow mustard and all the dirtiest shades of yellow, squirming all over their bodies as they dripped and wriggled and drooped. Tatters tore apart, fell to the floor, bloomed new figures that reached towards her, bits of dirt and dust that danced through the air. They were alive. Every inch of them was alive.

She turned to run but they surrounded her, bumping against her shoulders, and she couldn't scream, because when she opened her mouth spores flew inside, skin fluttered down her throat and their voices hitched and chiseled their way into her ears and she couldn't make out what they were saying, but it was all so curious, questioning, what what what why why why show us show us what is inside?

"Leave me alone!" Her words were unrecognizable, total nonsense, she choked and spat, fell to her knees, and they danced across her hands, gleaming fireflies that lit colored shadows across her arms. There was no way out but she crawled and they lifted her up with sticky flowing hands and she stumbled deeper into the school, pushed her way through the throngs of creatures and gasped and choked on their metallic dust and she pushed them away from her but they left a residue and the lockers glinted and the hallways opened and multiplied and the maddening *rrr? rrr? rrr?* and something squiggling down her throat released and burst and she fell again and colors burst behind her eyelids and she realized she was very late for class.

Oh god, she had wasted so much time crawling through these halls and thank God for her classmates, because they lifted her up with their gentle sweet hands and she didn't feel well, everything was shaky and blurry, but she had to get to class. Her classmates looked familiar unfamiliar as they thronged through the halls and it was a relief just to follow them deeper inside the school. Just follow. Just follow. They were quiet loud quiet inside her head, no one was talking out loud but she could still feel their questioning, and that was okay, she didn't know either but they all seemed to know where they were going as they ushered into classrooms and doors slammed shut and the hallways emptied out until it was just her and a few familiar unfamiliar faces, and so she followed them, and the hallway opened up and this must be her classroom, yes? This was where she was supposed to go.

They wrapped their arms around her, their hands were like clay, and she walked into the classroom and she was late and everyone was already sitting down and she was so embarrassed, the only place left to sit was on the big table and everyone was looking at her with their eyes no eyes and so she sat down and there weren't any seats at all, were there? No one else was sitting, they were all standing, they were all staring at her but their eyes didn't look right but that was okay.

She was tired. So when their flapping strange arms slid her back, cushioned her, urged her to lay down, she did. Stared up into the lights on the ceiling but they were too bright so she closed her eyes, but even with her eyes closed, she could see them staring down at her, faces blurred, asking questions that she couldn't understand and maybe didn't want to.

But they stroked her and reassured her and this was a funny sort of class but it was okay, their voices were low and comforting and she lay back back back and it didn't matter if her eyes were open or closed.

The lights weren't so bad. They were sort of nice. Four or five or eighteen classmates bustled around her, stroking her head, stroking her hands, asking questions always questions. There was a pressure against her hands as they were adjusted and pasted down into something sticky, and then her feet were spread apart and pasted down and she couldn't remember class ever being like this before but her thoughts kept drifting away and they kept asking their questions.

# THE WRITHING SKIES

Snip snip snip and a soft sound as her clothes fell away and five or ten or twenty classmates loomed above her and everything was okay so Sarah smiled.

# CHAPTER 9

**W**HY HAD SHE been so frightened of the lights? They were so relaxing, the way they blinked and moved and changed. There was nothing to be afraid of here. The chatter of her classmates was distant now. The lights flashed on off on, or was that just her blinking?

Sticky soft fingers pulled the clothes from her shoulders, and it was a relief. Everything had been filthy. Now she would be clean.

*Rrr? Rrr? Rrr?*

Everyone was so curious, and it was funny and Sarah would have laughed if she could move her mouth. She couldn't move at all, but she wouldn't let that bother her. She couldn't. Class was in session and she needed to be calm and still.

The air rippled around her.

One of her classmates, glowing yellow, a beautiful sun, fingers long and undulating, just like their coats. Their uniforms. Their . . .

Their fingers were pleasant, not painful, they slid beneath Sarah's temples, pushed their way through her soft skin, and massaged the muscle and tissue underneath. Hands everywhere, all at once. Sarah had never been this popular before.

The questions kept coming and she couldn't keep

up. She was bound to have trouble on the exam at this rate, but it didn't seem to matter.

The fingers massaged past the muscle, into her brain tissue, and poked and prodded and Sarah felt her legs twitch and more hands reached inside her. She was all lit up like an x-ray but that wasn't enough. Creeping slugs slid up her thighs, leaving sticky trails, and her cunt began to pulse and they attached to her clit, morphed and changed, slid into her hole and it felt so strange, thick but soft and pulsing.

Bursts of pleasure exploded in her temples as they wriggled deeper in. The pressure on her brain expanded contracted expanded contracted and the thing inside her moved in rhythm, in tandem, they worked together and the soft wet thing on her clit thrummed and she gasped when she came, it kept making her come, more than she could stand, and they kept asking, asking, asking.

Delicate fingers tweaked through her brain, looking for something, and Sarah remembered the way Derek's face fell, the way the look in his eyes changed and how he was suddenly someone she didn't know at all when she told him.

She had been so scared to tell him. Scared he wouldn't let her do what needed to be done. They couldn't keep it, she didn't want to keep it, but what would he say?

*"Are you sure it's mine?"*

And one of her classmates reached into her chest and felt the way her heart tore apart when he asked that, when he dared to ask that. They murmured and she kept remembering, couldn't stop now.

*"Of course it's yours. You're the only . . . "*

*"Well, how am I supposed to know that?"* She

*didn't know what to say, how to change his mind, how to make him hold her and comfort her. She needed his support, didn't he fucking know that? "Have you told anyone else?"*

*"Just Tiffany. I didn't mean to tell her. I couldn't help it. I had to tell someone." Maybe she should have told him first, but she just couldn't. "What would she do if he said he wanted to keep it? Tiffany heard everything first, always, and at least she had done something other than push Sarah away, at least she had listened and tried to help.*

*Blood rushed to his face then drained, leaving him pale and frightened-looking. "We can't let my dad find out. He'll lose it and poof, there's my job gone. There's everything gone. There's any chance at a future I might have had."*

*And she was relieved and mad because she was so glad he didn't want to talk her out of it but for fuck's sake why couldn't he just be nice to her? Tiffany had asked her what she thought he would say, and she didn't know, but she didn't expect this emptiness in his eyes.*

*"Stop crying, please, just stop crying. It doesn't help anything." The sound of his voice made the tears come harder, so she turned her face away.*

*Now the hard part. The really hard part. "They don't do it here, you know. We'll have to go to the city, and I don't have the money. How . . . "*

*He rolled his head back on his shoulders, stared at the sky. "Fuck. Look, this happened to my sister Sue before and I . . . I helped her. I know what we can do."*

Their fingers trailed down her chest, to her stomach, and slid in to the mess of flesh and tissue and glowing strangeness. It moved and tore and twined into their fingers and they shaped it and murmured and kept asking, asking, asking, but these questions sounded different. These questions felt different.

They stroked and cooed and they weren't questions at all, it was a lecture, the teacher droned about something and now they weren't helping anymore, they were hurting. They touched it, they touched the things inside her and their fingers were like knives, carving out spaces for it to grow and the pain snapped her back to the present.

It bubbled and burrowed and the calm sleepiness trickled away, and the lights blared down on her and she was waking up and all those faces staring down at her weren't so familiar after all and their questions didn't make sense and why were they touching her like this?

She struggled to sit up, and their hands moved, and they looked at her, their pale dumb faces so blank and curious, big wet eyes that hung empty in the writhing of their flesh, and she saw her stomach and it looked all mushed up, an exploded jellyfish and the scream ripped out of her throat and broke the spell and they hummed and muttered in a panic but they let her get up.

"Leave me alone!" She didn't know who she was talking to. Didn't matter. The door flopped open and she stumbled out into the hallway and the lights flashed yellow and orange and yellow and orange.

# CHAPTER 10

**T**HERE WAS NO one else in the hallway. Just the lights.

She must be late for class.

It was hard to breathe. Something stung in her stomach, but she didn't look at it, leaned against the hard shining metal of the lockers. It was freezing cold against her naked flesh, so cold it stung.

Had to get to class.

She pulled herself along the lockers. Classroom lights flickered ahead. She wouldn't' look out the window. The yard wasn't safe. There was something waiting outside, something hungry.

Where was everyone?

Was she dreaming?

She looked down at her wobbling, naked legs, *why was she naked*, and they gleamed with a light that didn't seem natural. Dreaming. She must be dreaming.

She needed to get to class. There was still . . . there was something important. Late. The bell rang shrill in her brain. Her stomach turned over, wailed, split and tore.

A classroom door opened ahead, and something beautiful streamed out of it, enticing, calling to her, and someone was asking questions and she should hurry up or she would be late late late.

# THE WRITHING SKIES

The men's bathroom door swung open as she passed, a terrifying blur of motion in all this silent atmosphere. The thing that came lurching out was covered in rot, the substance thick as jelly and Sarah could see her reflection pale and terrified in it. A snake of fear wound through her heart, tied up her feet and made her stumble.

"Sarah!" The voice was familiar enough to halt her run.

"Tiffany . . . ?" And yeah, beneath the goop that covered her face and hands and oh god, *everything*, those were Tiffany's eyes that peered out at her. "What happened?" Sarah wailed, and couldn't help herself, she touched her stomach, where that same substance burbled and infected and changed her.

"Get in here." Tiffany grabbed her, the slime slugged across her skin and Sarah wanted to pull away, but the lights pitter-pattered down the hall and she was starting to wake up, really wake up, the sound of Tiffany's voice brought her back to herself and they fell into the bathroom and braced their backs against the door.

The light in the bathroom was dim, the mirror smeared with more of the jelly. It was filthy in here, so unlike the gleaming surface of the rest of the school.

Sarah reached up to wipe her eyes, but her hands were smeared with the warm gel and she didn't want to touch her face with it. "Oh god, I'm so glad to see you," How long had it been since she had seen her friend? Had it really been since the camping trip, since—

Oh fuck, what was going on here?

Tiffany almost laughed, "As much of me as you can see under this shit, huh?"

"What *is* this stuff?"

"You've got it on you too. Sarah, where the fuck are your clothes?"

"I . . . they took them. Those . . . people out there. They took them and they were touching me."

"I hardly think they're people." Tiffany's voice was sharp, but Sarah heard the fear that shook under it.

"How did this happen? Why . . . ?"

"Fucking Derek. Fucking fuck."

"He's here too."

Tiffany rolled her eyes. "Yeah, I bet he is. Well, don't mind me if I don't go out of my way to help him. You're lucky I saw you. I've been stuck in here for . . . god, it feels like days, but it's hard to tell."

"I ran into him outside the school. Everything outside—"

"Yeah. I know. I couldn't stay in my room anymore. Mom was . . . I don't know where Mom is. There was something, but . . . not Mom. And then day wouldn't come and I could hear shit over here and my room . . . Well, I couldn't stay there anymore. There's a lot of fucked up shit going on, Sarah. I shouldn't have come in the school, but . . . have you heard their voices?"

"I think so. I heard something."

"They can be pretty persuasive."

"What did they do to you? What are they?"

Tiffany sighed. "You know as good as I do, kid."

"It's all my fault."

"No." Tiffany closed the space between them, wrapped her arms around Sarah's bare shoulders. "It's not your fault." The goo that grew from Tiffany's hand smeared down Sarah's back. She shivered. "Aw fuck, here, you're probably freezing. And if we're gonna get out of here, we can't have you running around totally naked." Tiffany removed her oversized hoodie, wincing as she stretched. She handed it to Sarah, but Sarah dropped it when she got a good look at Tiffany.

Clad only in a tank top, the glowing rot rippled, devastated all of Tiffany's visible flesh. She was absolutely covered in the shit. It crusted over in some places with a hard greenish shell. Rivulets of brackish water cascaded from deep set areas of the rot, thick black veins that bled down her shoulders.

"What did they do to you?"

"The same thing they did to you, I guess. Put the sweater on. We gotta get out of here."

"Where are we going?" Sarah pulled on the sweater. It was clammy and damp.

Tiffany shrugged. "I have no idea."

Fair enough.

"Derek's here, too. He went in one of the classrooms. I think."

"I don't give a fuck where Derek is, and you shouldn't either." Something must have passed across her face, because Tiffany softened. "Look, he wouldn't go hunting for you, I bet. I know that hurts to hear, but we have to count on each other, okay?"

"Can't we just . . . I just think we should stick together, that's all."

Tiffany raked a hand through her hair, and the goop adhered and clumped together, like some kind of disgusting hair gel.

"Okay, we'll see if we can find him, but I'm not making any promises. Let's . . . I don't know. Fuck. Let's head for the front door. We'll peek in the classes on the way and see if we see him. Okay? Sound like a plan?"

"Yeah." They had to find him. She couldn't just leave him here. She wouldn't. And Tiffany was wrong. He was probably looking for her right now. The sick feeling in her gut was just all this stuff that was going on. It had nothing to do with him. She edged the door open. "The hall looks clear, for now, at least. I don't suppose you have like . . . a weapon or anything on you?"

"Yeah, I have five guns stuffed in my pockets. Plus a machete." She paused. "Sorry. No. I got nothing. Wanna grab the back of the toilet? Maybe we can bash their brains in or something?"

Sarah considered, pictured herself wielding the porcelain rectangle like a baseball bat, splattering pale skin and luminescent globs of goo all over the place, one after the other. She shook her head. "No, I guess not."

"Okay, well. Let's get going then."

# CHAPTER 11

**THE LIGHTS IN** the hall flickered. The walls flexed. Tiffany plowed ahead with Sarah close behind her. They didn't speak. It was too quiet, even a whisper could draw attention to them. They headed towards the front of the school, and Sarah caught her reflection in the cold steel of the lockers, and the light that glinted off them started a headache somewhere deep inside, lit her up with pictures and sensations that she didn't want to focus on.

The hallways branched out endlessly. The lights made the path so confusing. The end of the corridor led to two more corridors, and they all looked the same. Doors everywhere, and the rustling behind them was manic. How would they ever find Derek? There were too many rooms to look in them all. She couldn't even call out to him. Tiffany's eyes were wide and frightened behind the mask of goop on her face, and Sarah's chest felt tight and panicky.

Sand poured from beneath the doors, shining, and things wriggled and changed within the dust. Derek had disappeared somewhere around here but there was no way to tell where. Was he still here? Was he okay? Was he worried about her? Even a little?

Sand pooled around their feet; no, mud, it was too sticky to be sand. They had to keep moving. Tiffany looked down a twisting hallway and nodded to Sarah. The mud sucked at her feet as she caught up. The front door, miles down the hall, dull and dented. They had to go.

"What about Derek?" At the sound of her voice, a murmur erupted behind them. Tiffany looked back again and twisting flesh tightened on her face, peeled her eyes wide open.

Stupid. She shouldn't have spoken aloud. Sarah didn't need to look back, she already knew, could already hear them, rustling, whispering, chattering. A yellowish glow highlighted Tiffany's face, tinted it sickening colors, and Sarah did not turn back, she would not turn back.

The classroom doors ahead of them swung open. All of them.

Figures bubbled out, dozens, hundreds, their heads inclined in a silent question, their bodies twisting and peeling and questioning and she wanted to feel fear, she should feel fear, but instead Sarah felt herself moisten and flush with heat.

*Rrr? Rrr? Rrr?*

Something inside her shifted.

Tiffany's face blossomed and changed, sprouted a fuzzy substance, scabs flaked off and revealed moving flesh beneath. Florescent light pulsed across the rivers and valleys of crust. "We gotta run." Her voice was changed. Husky. Her eyes shone.

Long, flopping fingers caressed the girls as they pushed past. The creatures stayed in place, but their hands reached out, groping, leaving shining oval droplets everywhere they touched. Sarah tried to brush away the drops, and they floated, tiny moons that circled her face, made flickering, dizzying revolutions. One burst against her lips and dribbled honey down her throat.

If it weren't for Tiffany's hand yanking her along, she wouldn't have been able to resist. Her classmates needed her, needed something from her. And the feel of their fingertips on her skin made heat rush between her thighs, made her drip lubrication and she could smell herself, musky and sweet and she felt so confused but Tiffany kept her moving, or she kept Tiffany moving, or they pulled each other along.

They couldn't run, the halls were too crowded, but the creatures didn't stop them, they didn't grab them, they just hung in the hallways, coming close, brushing against them, asking something over and over and over and she didn't know the answer, she had missed too much time, she would never pass and she was slowing down and Tiffany pulled her through.

The steel door to the outside was to their right, and they hadn't found Derek, hadn't even *looked,* but Tiffany dragged her towards it and Sarah didn't object, she couldn't, not anymore, they had to get out of here before it was too late.

When they passed the secretary's office, Derek tumbled out of the little alcove.

"Hey, wait!" He caught up to them.

"Derek!" His arm hung limp at his side, glowing and sticky, and he thrust it behind his back. His cheeks flared red, but his eyes flickered all over her face. "Were you just gonna leave me here?" His voice was a whine, and she felt disgusted—with him or with herself, she couldn't tell. Yellow light splashed his face. He looked sick.

*Rrr? Rrr? Rrr?*

"Keep moving!" Tiffany yelled.

# THE WRITHING SKIES

"Yeah, let's get out of here." They pushed through the door and into the fresh air outside.

# CHAPTER 12

**THE DUSTY AIR** was a relief. Sarah would have never thought she would be happy to see this endless grey night again, but after the artificial light of the school, it felt somehow safer.

"We've gotta barricade the doors. Don't let them out." Tiffany was breathless, her eyes glazed.

"With what?" demanded Derek. He gestured to the empty school grounds. Grass and glowing orbs and trees branches too thick to break. "Let's just get out of here."

Small, gelatinous blobs squeezed beneath the door. "Where do we go?" Inside, the creatures peered out windows, their eyes luminous with questions. Sarah shuddered. Bits of jelly clung to her skin.

Derek snarled. "I can't believe you guys were just going to leave me there."

"It didn't look like you were looking for us too hard."

"I didn't even know Tiffany was here."

The figures crowded at the windows of the school, peering out at them, flashing yellow orange yellow.

"We've gotta get out of here. You guys can fight later." Tiffany still wouldn't look at Derek.

"Well, where are we gonna go?" Sarah pressed her lips together.

There was nowhere to go.

"My place is close." Derek said.

"I couldn't get back in to my house once I left," Tiffany said. "Could you? Did you try?"

"I couldn't either. And . . . I was at your place, Derek. I was looking for you. I couldn't get in. And Mom's . . . "

"I don't know. What else are we gonna do? There's always the shed in my yard. I don't know, do you guys have any better ideas? I've got a bottle stashed there and I don't know about you two but I could use a fucking drink."

"Of course you want a drink. Just avoid your problems, right? Don't you think we should talk about what's going on here? About what happened?" Tiffany clenched her firsts, and something burst and dripped to the ground.

The school hummed. The doors vibrated with tension as the creatures huddled against the window. The bits of jelly on Sarah's arm pulsed in time with their humming. She 'tried to brush it off, but it clung firm to her skin. She wanted it off. She wanted it off right now.

"Can't it wait?"

"I don't think it fucking can."

"It can wait 'til we get somewhere safe and get a drink for fuck's sake. I'm not getting into this shit right now. Not in the middle of all this."

Sarah remembered the last time they drank. Her legs felt weak and she was spinning and all this was related somehow, and soon everything was gonna come out, and she wasn't ready for that, she would never be ready for that. "Honestly, I think I could use a drink too. Let's go."

Tiffany shrugged. Derek led the way.

Sarah dug her nail beneath the shining gel on her skin and peeled it off. It hissed and stung, but she tugged it off anyway. The crater it left behind was nauseating, and she tugged her sleeves down and concentrated on walking.

'The night was still around them. It was easy to imagine they could all just wander home, they were just out late after a long day at school and they could all go home to their warm safe beds and everything would be fine. As long as she didn't look too far up the street, as long as she didn't see them, skin twisting and glowing and silently ushering them in the right direction.

It was a good thing they were headed to Derek's place, because every other street was blocked with fluttering light. They didn't move, just watched. As if they were already going in the direction the things wanted them to go. Like they had no choice. Gleaming figures peeked from behind trees and around corners and Sarah didn't say anything over the lump in her throat.

Just walk.

She almost wished they would never get there. They could just stay in this state of transit forever, walking, mindless, not saying much, on a mission, because it felt like they were doing something and they didn't have to talk yet. They didn't have to do anything, don't think, don't speak, just walk.

But Derek's house wasn't far. He hurried up the broken stairs, hauled on the doorknob and it spun in place. "Fuck. Fuck, fuck, fuck. Nothing ever fucking goes right!" He pounded on the door, and the thud of his fist against the wood made Sarah wince. It was too loud.

"Stop." She touched his arm, gentle. He was damp. Clammy. He yanked away from her, but his face softened.

"Okay. We'll try around back. I'm sure we can get in the shed. I don't know. We need a few minutes to relax'. Calm down. I can't think out here."

The trees in the backyard loomed closer, bathing them in darkness. Sarah tried not to look too closely at the soft luminescence of insects that guided them forward. The shed opened, and they slipped inside. The dark corners were lit with a pale glow that shouldn't be there. The girls hesitated, but Derek went straight to a bench in the back and slipped his hand underneath, came out with a pack of smokes and a bottle of something. He slumped over on the bench, lit a smoke, took a swig, all in one fluid motion.

Sarah crept closer to Tiffany, took her hand. She needed to be near someone. They were all silent for a moment until finally Derek barked, "Close the door, Jesus Christ. Your eyes will get used to it." When he spoke again, his voice wasn't as gruff. "We don't want anything to know we're in here, do we?"

Tiffany moved away from Sarah and shut the door. As if it would make a difference. The glow dimmed, and Sarah waited for her eyes to get used to the gloom. Derek slouched in the corner, the bright light of his cigarette dancing like fireflies *no don't think about fireflies*. Sarah winced, and maybe Tiffany had the same thought, because she sighed. "We should talk about it, don't you think?"

"What's there to talk about?"

"She's right," Sarah's voice came out louder than she meant. "This all comes back to the . . . the trip, right? Do you think?"

"I don't know what you're talking about."

"We all saw it, Derek. It's the same—"

"I didn't see anything and the two of you were fucking drunk as shit. Whatever's going on out there has nothing to do with what we did. Even if it does come back to the trip, it's got nothing to do with *that,* okay? I don't need this right now. None of us do. It doesn't matter."

Sarah's stomach moved, flipped over, and she groaned. She could feel the heat of it against her hand, even through the heavy sweater. Hot as a fever. It pulsed and wriggled and made her feel sick, like she was ready to throw up.

"Are you okay?"

"I'm not sure."

"Is she okay?" Derek laughed. "I think you're the one who should be worried. What the fuck happened to you out there? I'm glad it's dark now, so I don't have to see that shit all over your face."

"You're one to talk. What's up with your arm, huh?"

"Shut up. Just shut the fuck up. You don't know what you're talking about."

Part of her stomach felt numb, dead, and beneath that, fresh hot pain. "I think I need to see what's going on. Do you have a flashlight?"

"I don't want you guys attracting attention."

"What fucking difference does it make?" Tiffany snarled. "You don't wanna talk, you don't wanna act, what do you wanna do? Sit in here and pretend nothing is happening?"

Sarah ran her hand along the top of the doorframe and found it. She flicked the flashlight on. Derek was framed in its light, and his face looked small and scared. The second the light was on him, he shoved his hand into his pocket, cigarette and all. A moment later, his other hand fished inside, retrieved the smoke. "What are you staring at?"

"Nothing." Sarah shone the flashlight towards her stomach, and lifted her shirt.

# CHAPTER 13

**F**OR A MOMENT, none of them spoke.

Her skin was distorted with bulging membranes, and everything was *moving*. Shining sacs distorted her body, and within the sacs, bright lights danced and moved. Veins like vines twisted and warped between the valleys of flesh, and pallid faces pressed against the skin of her stomach, impossible, fully formed. Yellow mucus dripped from swollen flesh and the mucus itself was alive, coursing through her skin, and as she watched, crusted scabs broke off, grew legs, dug deeper inside.

Pain wrenched through her as something sharp whipped against the inside of her flesh. It kneaded her skin, flapping and pulsing and it hurt the way it pressed against her. Inside her. Her hand, beyond her control, swatted at it, and it hissed, dove deeper into her stomach, out of harm's way, leaving behind unmoving rot and dripping liquid. It was somewhere deep inside her body now, out of sight.

"Oh what the fuck," Derek said. "That's not ... we ... "

Sarah sank to her knees. Debris and dirt from the floor stuck to her sweaty thighs. It was inside her. Whatever it was, it was inside her and it was living there. Her stomach was alive. A foreign invader, even worse than Derek's child, and what the fuck could they do with this one?

Derek stood up, and Tiffany stepped in front of Sarah. "Hey, wait a minute."

"I want it out," Sarah wailed. "Oh god, I want it out."

"We'll get it out, baby."

"Oh, just like the last time, huh?" Tiffany's voice cracked. She kept glancing back at Sarah.

"Yeah, just like the last time."

Oh god, if they had just done it right. If they hadn't been at the beach at just that moment. If they hadn't let all this happen. If they hadn't attracted attention. The thing inside her trembled and she pressed her hand to her stomach again and this time she felt something.

Something blossomed. Something changed.

Derek had a hammer. His hand pulsed with tangled veins. Tiffany was yelling something and it was too noisy and it was too much all at once.

"No," Sarah said. "No, never mind. Just. Let's just wait 'til morning. Let's sleep on it. I need to think."

Derek sneered. "Think about what? You wanna keep this one? Raise it as your own'? We don't have time to think it over. We gotta kill 'it. This will all go away. It all started with this, right? You see that?" He stepped forward, and Tiffany helped Sarah to her feet.

"How are you gonna kill it? It's all over her. It's inside her."

Derek held up the hammer. It looked heavy and wicked, the claw curved and sharp. He shrugged.

"Are you insane?" Tiffany demanded. "You'll hurt her. Do you even know what you're doing? Is this your solution to everything?"

"I'm doing what I have to do." Derek's voice broke. "This whole way through, I'm just doing what I gotta do. Sarah. My sister. We've gotta kill it. But we've really gotta make sure it's dead."

The movement in Sarah's stomach was nauseating. It was cold in the shed, but she felt warm. Too warm. She was so fucking sick of his excuses. "Oh right, your sister. That's where you got this brilliant idea in the first place. I guess it all went perfectly that time, did it?"

Derek backed away from them, lowered the hammer. "You know what happened. She was pregnant, I had to help her. I helped her."

"Why didn't she just get an abortion? Why didn't we just get an abortion?" What had she been thinking to listen to his insanity. "You knew it would be awful. You knew. If you did it to your sister . . . why did we trust you? Who gives a fuck if your dad finds out?"

Derek sat back down on the bench. "He'd kill me. Like, he really would have killed me, I think. After what happened with Sue. I fucked up, okay? I know that. I fucked up and I keep fucking up but we can still fix this. We gotta fix it." His voice broke as though he had been crying, but even in the darkness she could see that his eyes were dry.

"What happened with Sue?" Tiffany demanded. "It went fine with her, huh? You helped her out and the fetus just died and everyone lived happily ever after?"

Derek was quiet so long, Sarah began to think he wouldn't answer. "You think you wanna know the whole story? You think you wanna pry into this shit. It was mine."

"What?" Sarah's stomach stilled, listening.

"It was mine, okay? If you really wanna know, then let's rip this all wide open. It's all really fucked up and I didn't tell you because I didn't want to get into it—I don't like talking about this kinda stuff, Sarah. I thought we had a chance to get out of this. That's why I went back to school. And then I met you. We coulda gotten out of here and gotten away from all this, Sarah, but you had to get pregnant."

"Excuse me—"

"What are you talking about?" Tiffany was the only one who sounded calm.

"My dad is a piece of shit. I know it, you know it, and it was his fucking fault in the first place."

Something dripped inside Sarah's stomach, spilling into her lower abdomen, creating a horrid pressure against her bowel.

"You think you're the only one shitty things happen to, Sarah?" He laughed, but it sounded mean. "You two have no idea the kind of things that can happen. The kind of things your family can make you do."

"He's just trying to make us feel bad," Tiffany didn't sound sure of herself.

"Want proof? If we ever get inside, I'm sure there's still some tapes around. Sold most of 'em, but I imagine he kept a few for himself, sick old pervert. He started when I was 9. Sue was 15. Figured I was too young to get her pregnant I guess, but he was greedy and he kept us going at it until things got a little tricky."

Everything inside Sarah was cracking open. She knew she needed to say something, but she didn't know what, she could barely process anything with her guts ripping open and dribbling over the floor.

"I'm sorry, Sarah," Derek sounded far away. "He made me do it. He made me hurt her. He made me hurt you, because I didn't know what else to do, all I could think of was the way he looked at Sue when he found out, and then he showed me how to get it out of her." He got off the bench, moved closer. His eyes danced with sadness or fear or anger, she couldn't tell which. The hammer was still in his hand. "There's no good solutions, okay? But we gotta do something."

""'Get away from her!"

An ocean moved inside her. Something dripped between her thighs. Pearlescent drops fell to the ground, crawled away. She reached towards her stomach, and just like that, one of the membranes burst, and a rush of liquid splashed and the sac emptied and something crawled through her pubic hair, liquid quick, slithered in. Sarah gasped as it tangled its way inside her.

"Oh fuck, what is it doing? What is that?"

A glowing thread of mucous, whipping like an eel, dangled from between her thighs. Her hand passed through the gunk when she tried to yank it out. It slid further up inside her, thickened and hardened, and Sarah fell to the floor, legs splayed out.

The end inside her stayed hard, and the end that dangled out of her split into dozens of gummy strands that wrapped 'round her legs, her thighs, inched up beneath her shirt. It thrummed inside her and her eyes rolled back in her head, she couldn't help it, she couldn't stop it. Tiffany was yelling, trying to pull it out of her, but it was too late, too late, too late.

Her body lit up and the light was so bright she couldn't see her friends, only hear them screaming. Arcs of light expanded, soft and protective, and the hum began and she couldn't see out, she couldn't see anything, but she didn't need to anymore.

She felt fine.

Before it had been an awful scary thing, but she could feel it inside her now, the way it stroked her from the inside out, it pressed against her insides and released a scent like honey like fresh sweet grass and it kept asking questions questions questions as it explored. It flowed through her body, liquid and tingling and it pressed against her heart and the inside of her skin and she felt much, much better. She felt safe. The panic that flooded her brain was no match for the tentacles of calm that wound their way inside and it wasn't the same as last time, it was something else, and it pressed against her and she pressed back, and suddenly she wasn't sure.

It wanted her to feel safe. It wanted her to feel good. It wanted to know her, to know her better than anything had ever known her before.

It wanted to know them all.

Soon.

The bubble popped.

Tiffany and Derek were screaming and Derek had the hammer but he was not coming any closer. Sarah sat up.

"Are you okay? Oh god, what the hell just happened?" Tiffany touched Sarah's stomach, a trail of slime stuck to her hand.

"What should I do? How do we kill it?" Derek hovered a few feet away.

"It's gone inside. I don't think we can do anything. It's okay."

"'Whatever. Fine. Let's just all die here then." Derek took another swig from his bottle and turned away from them, cradling his hand. It looked worse, if that was possible. "Who's first? Tiffany? You're not looking too good. How's it feel having that stuff all over you?" He burped.

"I'm fine." Every time she moved her mouth, more sores opened up, leaked phosphoresce.

"None of us are fine!" He stomped over towards them, waved his arm under their noses. It smelled putrid. "Does this look fucking fine to you?"

"Stop it! Just stop it!"

"You're one to fucking talk. We've gotta get that shit out of you. We've gotta get it off us all."

*"How?"*

He shook his head. "This isn't my fault. Don't yell at me. Jesus Christ." He grabbed Tiffany's shoulder, his thumb dug into the goop and she *screamed* and fell to her knees as something on her shoulder cracked and burst and Tiffany would never scream like that and oh god, Sarah had been so selfish. She wasn't the only one in pain.

"Stop it!" She grabbed Derek's arm, the good one, and yanked. "Leave her alone!"

He whirled, his eyes sharp. "You're both so fucking stupid." For a minute, she thought he was going to hit her, and she braced herself for it. Instead he winced, and there was a plop plop plop as something dripped from his arm to the ground. He closed his eyes, shook his head. "I'm sorry. I'm sorry, we're all such a fucking mess. This is a mess. I can't handle it anymore." He slumped back on the bench, back to the bottle.

Sarah turned. "Are you okay?" Tiffany nodded, but she wouldn't meet Sarah's eyes.

'What the fuck were they going to do?

"Derek . . . " He didn't turn to look at her, and she didn't know what she wanted to say anyway. Tiffany crouched on the floor, her eyes distant.

She couldn't think about all that shit with Derek and his sister. She couldn't think about what was going on outside the shed. She didn't want to think about what was going on inside her body, but she could still feel it moving, somewhere deep inside her. This was exhausting. Too much. She pressed her forehead against the shed wall and closed her eyes.

It didn't take Derek long to fall asleep. He could never handle his booze, or maybe it was the stress, or maybe he was just ignoring them. He curled up on the floor, turned away from the girls, letting the silence speak his anger. Sarah fidgeted, worried the bottom of the sweater between her hands. The silence growing between her and Tiffany was almost as bad as the silence from Derek. Could he really be mad at them? How could any of them be mad in a situation like this? They needed to stick together, didn't they?

Eventually, Tiffany nudged Sarah. She looked almost normal in the darkness. From outside, the quality of the shadows was changing. The lights were changing. Tiffany nodded to the door and Sarah glanced at Derek. Tiffany was right. They needed to talk for a minute, and there was no way they were getting any talking done here. Not with Derek's attitude. They needed to figure it out themselves, and then fill him in and talk him into whatever they decided. Maybe if they could come up with a good plan, he wouldn't be mad anymore.

Sarah was so tired of people being mad at her.

The door whispered open. Sarah stepped outside

first, yanking the sweatshirt down over her bottom, ignoring the way her stomach twisted and ached.

The air smelled of salt. The grass moved beneath her feet. Tiffany slid the door shut.

Something that was not the moon rose in the sky, and a sickening orange light illuminated the backyard. Neither girl dared look up. They kept their heads bent low, focused on the writhing grass. It glowed a dull brown, moved like worms, hundreds of worms twining around each other, chewing mulch and dirt. The houses that surrounded them looked false, rudimentary shapes sketched by an inexperienced artist. The windows blinked open like eyes. They ducked beneath a cardboard cutout of a tree deep in the backyard. It did nothing to offer them cover. Sarah still felt incredibly exposed.

Tiffany's eyes were wide and panicked, her breath raspy and quick. Sarah had thought nothing could scare her, but that was ridiculous. Tiffany had every right to be just as afraid as anyone else.

"What are we going to do?" Her voice was garbled. When she opened her mouth, Sarah could see the way the strands of goop wound down her throat. "We have to get away from him. Fast."

"We can't. I know he's volatile, but he's just scared. Like us. And what about his sister? His dad? After what his dad did to him . . . "

'A sudden cramp and the blood rushed away from her face. A sound like a balloon popping, and fluid spilled from her waist. Sarah wobbled, fell to her knees. At the same time, Tiffany gasped, and her hand fluttered to her face, her shoulders, her arms, where the rot bubbled and twisted deeper inside.

The strange substance that leaked over their flesh

stung and fizzled and screamed to the sky. And the sky murmured in response. The yellow bled to orange, to red.

It saw them. It definitely saw them. It had known they were there all along. Razor-sharp pain shot through Sarah's skull. Derek was screaming, and part of her wanted to go to him, to make sure he was okay, but the other part cradled her stomach where it burbled and the sound of his voice did not invite sympathy, it pushed her away. It wasn't hurt. It was *angry*.

Her skin was crawling. The things inside it bulged and warped, wide awake now. Soft slugs dripped to the ground from her cunt, trailed through the grimy earth. More sounds came from the shed. Wood cracking. A bottle shattered. Derek was furious—if he was feeling the same pain they were, he was not taking it sitting down. The door swung open and she loved him, she couldn't help fucking loving him, but she wasn't ready to see him. She wasn't ready to solve this with him. Tiffany was right. She wouldn't let him decide for her this time.

Tiffany crouched on the ground, holding her head in her hands, teeth gritted against the pain. Beneath the scum on her skin, shapes wormed—not the size of Sarah's burden, but alive. Oh, definitely alive. Sarah grabbed her wrist and a gritty layer of skin sloughed off in her hand. She pulled Tiffany to her feet and they slipped through the fence, hobbled into more dark backyards.

It didn't hurt so much while they were moving.

# CHAPTER 14

**T HE AIR WAS** so thick. A few yards away, they had to stop to catch their breath. Strange organic shapes cast unsteady shadows. Something moved behind the windows but hell, what difference did it make? It didn't matter where they went. They were coming closer to the truth and there was nothing they could do to stop it.

"They're what we saw at the beach." Tiffany nodded towards the window. "I mean, it's pretty fucking obvious. We weren't that drunk. I know what we saw."

"Yeah." Sarah still couldn't look at the sky, couldn't confirm those writhing lights and what they all might mean. "Is it because of what we did? Do you think? Or just . . . wrong place, wrong time?"

Tiffany shrugged. "Both?"

"I'm sorry . . . "

"Hell. How's your stomach?"

Sarah lifted her shirt. Her smooth abdomen had swollen and grown taut. It glowed like a moon, a soft light emanating from the orb of her stomach. A crescent shape arced underneath, and long tentacles of fingers twisted through the layers of skin. Scabs flaked away and beneath, wormy new meat grew. She tasted bile deep in her throat. The tentacles waved, broke skin, dripped pus, and Sarah yanked her shirt back down. Timid fingers poked their way past her tight stomach, down into her pelvis, wrapping around the bone, and Sarah groaned. It ached deep inside her, everywhere. Was it writhing deeper, or ready to escape?

Tiffany retched and ripped Sarah's attention away from herself. Hunks of dry, stringy flesh flaked from her shoulders, revealing the raw meat that lay beneath.

"Oh, Tiff . . . "

Tiffany pressed her lips together, opening more sores around her mouth. Her eyes watered with pain, and her hands gestured uselessly at her body. Little choking noises bubbled from her throat, and she rasped and coughed and tears leaked and finally she spat out something fat and orange that wiggled away. Shook her head, closed her eyes. "It fucking hurts," she nearly laughed. "God, it fucking hurts so much."

Sarah wailed. What was wrong with her? Caught up in her own shit when Tiffany was the one in real pain here. Tiffany was the one who was really suffering.

"I'm so sorry. I should never have dragged you into this."

"Not your fault. Fucking Derek's idea."

"No . . . "

Still her fault. What the fuck had she been thinking? She let him make all the decisions. He sounded right. He sounded reasonable. They couldn't afford an abortion and they couldn't afford to ask for help. She hadn't even been supposed to tell Tiffany, but how the fuck could she keep it from her best friend? Tiffany had known something was up before she even told her, and Sarah was so sick and so nervous about Derek's plan that she asked Tiffany to come. She didn't tell her, not all of it, not then. Once she was there, she would have to help. Sarah needed her. Tiffany had hated Derek by this point, of course she did, but she came. But only because she didn't know what she was getting herself into. Sarah barely knew what she was getting them into. She had trusted him, and wasn't that a laugh? Wasn't that just the pinnacle of wishful thinking?

But he had done what he said he would do.

He took care of it.

# CHAPTER 15

## BEFORE

**T**HEY ACTED LIKE it was a party. Sarah had expected to be the drunkest. She needed it the most and hell, it wouldn't hurt anything at this point. But she couldn't. Her nerves were too jittery, and every sip of whiskey wound its way straight to the bottom of her stomach and sat there unpleasantly. Tiffany and Derek drank more. Especially Derek. Tiffany held her liquor well, but she was quiet, staring at the sky. Derek sure wasn't quiet. Was he nervous? He wasn't acting like it. He was laughing and smoking. They all were. Acting like they were just here for fun.

"I don't suppose anyone checked the weather report before we left?" Practically the first words Tiffany had spoken, and Derek laughed too hard.

"What do I look like, a weatherman? Oooh, it's supposed to get foggy around midnight with mild showers." Liquid from his plastic cup sloshed onto the sand.

Sarah followed Tiffany's gaze to the sky. "Why, do you think it's going to storm or something?"

'It should be much darker by now, but echos of sunset lingered. The colors were all wrong. Blue and green and yellow, swirled together in Rorschach shapes that made her dizzy. Maybe she *had* been drinking too much.

"The stars don't seem right, do they?"

"What are you, high or something? The stars don't seem right? Fuck, we haven't even smoked up yet." Derek's laughter veered into hysterical, but it didn't seem so funny to Sarah. "I'll be right back, gotta drain the beast."

Sarah shuffled closer to Tiffany, forced a smile. Tiffany's eyes were hard and she didn't smile back. "I'm starting to have second thoughts."

Yeah, Sarah was too. And here it was. This was her out. This was her chance to say no. Wasn't that why she brought Tiffany, anyway? In case she needed a reasonable voice? In case things got out of control? But even if the words were close to her lips, even if she was sober as fuck *could she really be sober if the stars were spinning like that*, she still couldn't quite get the words out. "No, please. I need you to stay. You don't have to do anything. Just be here. Please?"

Tiffany didn't say anything, and a star fell from the sky. Sarah watched its path, and even after it disappeared, she could see the light dance in her vision. When Tiffany finally spoke again, Sarah jumped. "I don't know if I can. There's gotta be a better way to do it. Like, a pill or something?"

Panic rippled through Sarah's chest. Yeah, maybe there was, but that meant doctor appointments and telling her mom and buying the prescription and she didn't want to wait. It was too late to change the plan. Way too late.

She didn't want to fight about it. It was time to get it over with. She had been on pins and needles all week, and the longer they waited, the worse it got. Her stomach was swollen, and soon people would start noticing. Soon it might really be too late.

No. She was going to wake up tomorrow and this would all be over with. She could start forgetting any of this had ever happened.

She'd never talk Derek into doing this another way. Not after all this.

No matter what Tiffany thought, Derek was a good guy. He was right. This was just a fucking real bad situation, and maybe he wasn't handling it well, but who was? Sarah had been crying herself to sleep for weeks, and after this went away, after it was over and done with, things could get back to normal. She imagined better trips this summer, just her and Derek, being together the way they had been before all this started.

"I just wanna get it over with," she said, and Derek came back. He looked different. Still drunk, but not as happy. Distant.

"Yeah, it's time." He glanced at Tiffany, saw the change in her face. "No backing out now—okay, girls? This is gonna suck for a few minutes, but then it'll all be over with." He crouched next to Sarah, stroked a strand of hair out of her face. "I'm so proud of you for doing this. I don't want to hurt you, and if there was any other way, you know I'd do it, right?"

"I don't feel good about this. I think we should go. Something doesn't feel right." Tiffany didn't sound sure. Most of the fight was out of her. It was getting dark now, fast.

Derek's eyes flashed and before he could say anything, Sarah said, "Please, this is what I want, okay?"

"Yeah, come on, Tiffany. It's me doing all the

work." He looked at Sarah. "I rolled a joint. It'll be good for the pain."

Sarah hated getting high. It always made her paranoid but right now she felt ready to jump out of her skin, she just wanted to not be herself at all. She should have drank more. She wished she were blackout drunk, and then none of this would matter.

Derek lit a joint. He passed it to Sarah first and she inhaled, let the smoke fill her lungs, felt everything in her body relax. She listened to the ocean, lapping peacefully nearby. The stars were blurry now. They reflected on the waves, looked like an ocean full of luminescent jellyfish winking back at her. She exhaled and coughed, but Derek kept smiling at her and she passed the joint to Tiffany.

This would be over soon.

Derek stood up. "Maybe you should take your shorts off. You don't wanna get them all full of blood or whatever." The thought of blood made her feel a little weak. This was gonna be bad'. Her head was pounding and maybe smoking a joint wasn't such a good idea after all, but Derek was smiling at her. He was trying his best. Tiffany didn't look happy. She didn't want either of them to be unhappy. She turned away. She didn't want them looking at her, not until this was all over with.

She unbuttoned her shorts and let them slide down to her ankles, stepped barefoot into the sand. Her oversized sweatshirt covered her ass, covered her bulging stomach. If she had waited any longer, there would be no hiding it.

Tiffany's eyes were bloodshot. She picked up Sarah's shorts, folded them, looked back to the sky. "Guys, how . . . are you sure you're' not going to hurt her?"

"It'll be fine. Same as with Sue. Kinda the same. It's not a big deal. It'll be fine."

Sarah took a deep breath. Her arms were trembling. She didn't want to show it, didn't want them to know she was scared. Tiffany would never go along with this if she knew how scared she was. Derek wouldn't like it. No. They needed to get this over with.

"Okay." Her voice was too bright, too cheerful, and it made her wince. "Okay, let's do this. 'I just—I just want it out. Let's get it out."

Tiffany pressed her lips together. "What do you want me to do?"

"Can you hold her? Just . . . keep her steady. I think it's easier if we're standing. Uh. I don't know." A sheen of sweat broke out on Derek's upper lip and Sarah didn't want to see that. She didn't want to hear the nerves in his voice, because she knew they were all on the brink of something and it would be so easy right now to change her mind, but then everything would change and from here there was no going back.

"Yeah, that's fine. Yeah. Tiffany, just, just kind of hold me steady."

Tiffany came behind Sarah, looped her arms around her waist, knotted her hands above Sarah's bulging stomach. It pressed out against her sweatshirt, round as a moon. Sarah still felt nothing for it. This wasn't how this all should go down, the sweat under her arms told her that, but it was okay. It was the right choice, even if it wasn't the right way to go about it.

It would be over soon.

Derek made eye contact, just for a moment, then he took another swig of whiskey and he swung. He didn't ask if she was ready. His fist hit like a brick.

Sarah had never been punched before, had never been in a fight. It ripped the breath out of her. Her legs buckled, but Tiffany held her up and that "ooff" sound that fell from her mouth did not seem like hers, did not sound familiar at all. The pain shot through her like an arrow. Stars lit up in her vision like fireflies. No, not fireflies. Not quite.'

"Fuck, fuck, Sarah, are you okay?" Tiffany blurted. Derek didn't stop.

"Shut up, she's fine, it's too late, we gotta keep going." He hit her again.

"Sarah!"

"I'm fine," she gasped, and the pain flowed, and they kept going, Derek's fist pounded against her gut and whatever was inside rattled back, and it hurt so much, so much more than she thought it would. The pain ripped through her stomach, into her back, her heart, her pelvis. Everything inside her ripped apart and those lights flashed in front of her eyes.

*Fireflies.*

*I'm okay I'm okay I'm okay.*

He hit her again. Sarah's hair was wet with Tiffany's tears, and it was too late now, they had to keep going.

Someone was screaming and it wasn't her.

He hit her again and when would this ever end would this even fucking work what had they been thinking?

He hit her again and she rolled her eyes to the sky, and the stars shook and Tiffany was saying something but she couldn't make it out. She was asking something and he hit her again and something broke and Sarah screamed, she couldn't stop, it poured out of her as something deep inside erupted.

Her legs shook and melted. She fell. The sand was soaked and sticky with the fluid that leaked from between her legs.

Derek brushed hair back from his face. "Fuck, lift her up, we're not done yet, we gotta make sure."

"How can you be sure?" Tiffany screamed. "What the fuck else can you do?"

"I don't know!"

"Ugh . . . " The cramps were worse than anything she had ever felt. Her head was huge, swollen, floating. She tried to stand up but toppled forward, onto her hands and knees.

"It's not even blood! We're not done!"

"Fuck! Sarah, are you okay?"

And that was ridiculous, of course she wasn't okay. Inside her, something rippled and moved and yanked and she screamed and Derek screamed.

"We're not doing this for nothing! It's too late to stop!" He rolled her over on to her front and there was no warmth in his eyes and she tried to breathe and tried to tolerate it and she couldn't she couldn't couldn't.

*It's okay it's okay it's okay it's okay it's almost over.*

And Derek kicked her in the gut and kicked her again and he stomped on her stomach and finally, finally the blood came and it was a release but the pain didn't stop it just kept crashing waves of blood and please, please let it be over.

She couldn't breathe. 'It hurt too much. Something wasn't right inside her. Worse, something wasn't right in the sky.

Tiffany and Derek were screaming at each other, Tiffany was pulling him away and she was hitting him and in the sky a hazy beam of light opened in the clouds and the fireflies poured out, chittering, and behind them . . .

Something massive was up there.

Then Tiffany was helping her up, muttering something about the salt water, and they stumbled in and the salt water wasn't going to help, oh no, not now. Her legs were covered in blood and the blood soaked the water around them and the thing in the sky was getting closer.

Tiffany was saying something but Sarah couldn't hear her, not over the static in her ears and not over the lights in the sky. Blue green yellow orange red red red and from above, a huge shining orb lit the sky, it was the moon it wasn't the moon it was all wrong.

It exploded.

Beams of scattered light curled through the sky, gigantic phosphorescent worms. Glittering dust fell, coated their shoulders. Tiffany was crying and Derek was running, running to the woods, but he didn't get far, because *they* came out of the woods, they tumbled down in beams of light and there were thousands of them and they were gibbering and asking questions and they sounded excited and curious and they had so many questions.

*Rrr? Rrr? Rrr?*

The sky opened. Everywhere. Darkness peeled back, revealed thousands of shining eyes glowing and blinking blue green yellow orange red red red red and all those eyes stared down at them and they kept asking their incessant questions

*Rrr? Rrr? Rrr?* and it was too loud and Sarah clamped her hands to her ears and she turned to run, but they were surrounded, and they were pushing

Derek into the ocean and they were *everywhere*, there were hundreds of them, figures made of glinting light and desperate curiosity.

Sarah surrendered.

Closer.

Fluttering appendages touched her hair and face, whisper soft. They wiped away her tears, tasted them.

Fingers slid deep inside her, so deep, and she trembled and the pain went away and the bleeding stopped.

They held her and touched her and kissed her everywhere it hurt and they asked questions she didn't know the answer to and they kept falling from the sky.

She didn't know who she was while she was in their arms. Everything was liquid and pleasure and she was laughing and the sky was blinking down at her and a black gaping hole opened directly above them, a dark opening where no light shone out and rows and rows of hungry teeth glinted and the creatures chittered and Sarah laughed because they weren't done yet, they still had so much to learn.

They pulled her from the water and now she could hear Tiffany and Derek moaning too but she wasn't jealous, she didn't mind, because their slithering tongues lapped inside her and tentacles explored her brain and squeezed things out of her a drop at a time. They flickered over her stomach and they seemed so excited and she was excited too and it made her so happy to let them see what was inside.

They reached in her brain and looked at her memories and licked them and sucked them and she lived it over and over again and they asked questions questions questions and they touched inside her cunt and they touched inside her gut and they touched where the baby had been, had never been, had never really been and the mouth in the sky opened wider wider wider and the lights reached down and then Sarah was flying, she was flying into the mouth but it wasn't chewing, even though she could feel how hungry it was and soon she would give herself to it, yes, yes, but it had so much it needed to ask her and it wanted to see everything and that was fine and they all flew into the mouth in the sky and came out the other side and it was flashing blue green yellow orange red and blue green yellow orange red red red red red.

# CHAPTER 16

## BEFORE

**S**ARAH WOKE UP SCREAMING.

"What the fuck! Shut up, shut up!" Derek was as pale as the sand that surrounded them. Sarah grabbed her stomach, grabbed handfuls of sand. It didn't hurt anymore, thank fuck, but what the fuck, what the fuck had happened?

"Where—" She gasped.

"Calm down, Jesus Christ."

"The sky, the things in the sky, oh god, where are we? Are we okay?" Tiffany stood up, sat back down in the sand. Her hands clambered over her own body. "What the fuck happened?"

"Apparently you can't hold your liquor, Jesus Christ." Derek's eyes searched the sky, only for a moment, yanked them back to the ground. He lit a cigarette and coughed as he exhaled.

"No, what? What?" Sarah still couldn't breathe. She glanced at the sky and the eyes weren't there, weren't looking at her, but she could feel them and she couldn't look and they were all in the sand. They were here. They were in the sand.

"I guess we just fell asleep last night after. After. God. I don't remember much of anything. It's over though, right? We did it? It went fine, just like I said it would."

"Guys, no, it didn't go right. What happened?" Sarah couldn't look back up at the sky. The beach was empty, clear. They were okay. Right? They were okay.

"Nothing happened." Derek wouldn't meet her eyes.

Tiffany was crying. "I wanna go home, okay? Let's just go home."

"What fucking happened?"

"I agree. Let's go home. We all need some rest. Nothing happened, Sarah. We did it." He pulled her into a hug, damp and sweaty. "It's fine. Let's just go. Let's get out of here."

They packed in silence and Sarah's heart pattered in her chest and nothing was the right color, was it? The sky was blue but the sun wasn't out, the sky wasn't right and it would be better if she just didn't look at it at all, wouldn't it? Yeah, it would be better when she got home and got a good night's sleep and then things could get back to normal. It was a traumatic night and they smoked too much and drank too much and finally they piled into the car and if there was no one else on the streets, that was just because it was too early, so early and when they finally rounded the street to Sarah's apartment she could just weep from relief and she kissed Derek goodbye and he didn't meet her eyes and she went inside and stayed there for a long time.

# CHAPTER 17

## NOW

ORANGE LIGHT PULSED rhythmically from the sky and they hid, or tried to, shuffled behind twisted shapes and bulging shadows'.

"Where the fuck are you guys?" Derek, a yard or two over, screaming. Scared.

Tiffany put her hand over Sarah's mouth and they locked eyes. She couldn't help it. She felt bad for him. Yeah, he was awful, but she sure as hell wouldn't want to be alone right now either. She pushed Tiffany's hand away. """We can't leave him alone out here like this."

"Are you serious Sarah? After all this, you still wanna help that asshole?" Beneath the cracking sores on her face, Tiffany didn't look angry. Just tired.

"He's not an asshole, he's just fucked up. We all are. Hell, he has more of a reason to be than we do, after what his dad did."

Tiffany held her eye. "Even if that's true, it's no excuse. Half the shit he says is a lie. Besides, if he did that to Sue, he knew how hard it would be, he knew it would hurt you - and what the fuck did he think he was doing with that hammer?"

Sarah swallowed, and her thoughts swirled and there were no answers, there were just specks of light, miniscule insects that glowed and pulsed, danced around them, excited. "Aw, fuck, let's get moving, please." But the insects followed them, illuminated them and Derek couldn't miss them now, and this was pointless, wasn't it? Where could they go?

They ran into the street. They were coming, they were everywhere, blobs of orange that swirled with energy, poured out of backyards, stayed just out of reach. They may as well be arrows pointing directly at them. There was nowhere to hide. Derek was at the top of the street, briefly silhouetted in darkness, and then he was stumbling toward them.

"Fuck." There were tears in Tiffany's eyes, and Sarah wanted to hug her, but she was afraid she would just hurt her friend more. "What's the point? We're fucked." Tiffany's shoulders slumped. Fireflies buzzed around her head.

"What the fuck, why did you guys leave me back there? Where do you think you're going?" His eyes shook and tears dribbled down his cheeks.

"Fuck off. You know why." Tiffany was defiant, but Sarah couldn't help it. She hated to see him like this—he tried to stay so tough all the time but the bags and tears under his eyes told the truth. She didn't want to love him, but she just fucking did. She wrapped her arms around him, pressed her cheek against his.

"I'm sorry, I don't know. This is all so fucked up."

The thing in her gut wriggled and Derek pulled away from her. "Let me see it."

"No . . ."

"Sarah, let me fucking see it." And he ripped the sweatshirt up and the creatures bulged out and twisted at the sound of his voice. The membrane that held them in was so thin now. Misshapen. Awful.

Sarah groaned at the sight of it and Derek smacked her across the face. She fell, scraping her knees on the pavement.

"You dirty slut."

She looked up at him and something leered at her from the orange sky.

"It was probably never mine in the first place. You got us all infected with this shit. It's your fault! None of this is my fault. You and Tiffany are fucked, you've got it all over you, I shouldn't even be here. I don't wanna be here."

"Fuck you, Derek."

"Fuck me?" He whirled on Tiffany, and she grabbed his forearm, shoved his hand in front of his face.

"What the fuck is this then? If you're not part of it, if it's not your fault, what the fuck is this?"

Orange lights swarmed his hand *rrr rrr rrr* not questions, knowing, and his hand was destroyed, rotting, utterly covered in the stuff, but it was not growing, it was dying, it was putrid.

"This?" He waved his hand and bits of flesh blobbed off it, dripped to the ground. "This is sure as hell not my fault. I touched Sarah and now my hand is fucked. She's diseased. I dunno what the hell happened to you, Tiffany, but I guaren-fucking-tee it didn't come from me."

"Oh my god," said Sarah. The tears in his eyes did not elicit her sympathy anymore, they just made her sick. "You fucking asshole."

He shook Tiffany off. "Fuck you too, Sarah. This is all because of you. If you hadn't gotten knocked up, we would never have been there, and we wouldn't be dying out here! We wouldn't be fucking rotting alive."

"Takes two to tango," but she said it quiet, and couldn't stop the tears from coming.

"Let's get out of here," Tiffany begged.

"We can't. What can we do?"

Derek closed his eyes, pained. "I'm sorry. My temper . . . I know. I know it's wrong. Let me see your stomach again. That's where the problem is. We gotta . . . we gotta do something."

"No." She moved closer to Tiffany.

*Rrr? Rrr? Rrr?* It was maddening, excited, screaming in her ears. *Rrr? Rrr?*

"Let me fucking see it!" He moved too fast, tore the sweater as he yanked it away from her gut. Sarah tripped, fell back on the pavement, banged her head painfully.

"Get away from her," Tiffany screamed, but the scabs tightened and her movements were stiff, not as fast as his.

Derek kneeled over Sarah, face twisted in disgust. "We've gotta kill it. All of it this time." Sarah couldn't look at him, couldn't look at anything, not the sky, not her stomach, not her friends. The things moved through her skin, peeled through muscle, ripped membranes and tore through something inside her. How could they kill it? It was everywhere.

Derek picked up a hunk of concrete from the ground and Tiffany ran at him and Sarah closed her eyes, but the screaming wasn't Tiffany, the screaming was static and it ripped through her entire body, the screaming was *blue green yellow orange red* because the sky had opened its eyes again.

# CHAPTER 18

**T**HEY HAD ITS ATTENTION.

Eyes and eyes and eyes opened, peeled back reams of darkness and bulged out, agog, staring into their souls. The mouth opened, slow, so fucking slow. Buzzing lights swarmed out, undulating worms of yellow and orange and pulsing red. Derek and Tiffany were gone, she couldn't see them, everything was just light and motion and calming words thrumming through her ears.

*Rrr rrr rrr.*

She was too tired to move. There was no running any more.

They swam inside and kissed her and buzzed and rippled and if they wanted to take her apart, so be it. If they wanted to put her back together, good luck to them.

Everything tingled, lips, toes, hair, everything buzzed with motion and questions and she was so fucking tired of their questions, so tired, and her closed eyelids did nothing to fight off the glare, and even if they did, the tiny fireflies slipped inside to kiss the globes of her eyes and soft flexible fingers slid inside her ears and she couldn't hear she couldn't see she couldn't move, her hands were stuck in soft tingling muck and the only thing that she could move was whatever the fuck was growing inside her stomach, that didn't stop moving, that was full of motion and ready to burst and she just wanted it to be over.

Slimy soft tickled the inside of her ears, slid out, left behind a thick residue.

She could hear again.

Something was coming down the street. Distant, rumbling. She wasn't afraid anymore. She didn't feel anything anymore. Just calm. Peaceful. Tired. So tired.

It was getting closer, whatever it was.

They slid out from her eyelids, and she could see again, a little.

The tingling stopped.

Sarah sat up. Her teeth chattered and she couldn't stop shaking. Cold.

The questions were still coming. They never stopped. Hundreds of small wet mouths kissed her all over, things wriggled in her throat, released honey and it was okay. They kept asking asking asking but they wanted her to be comfortable, they wanted to lull her off to sleep and of course she would let them because they only had her best interests at heart. And Derek was speaking and Tiffany was speaking but they were far away and they were calm and dreamy and everything felt so good, they knew just how to touch her, they knew just what she needed.

The pain in her stomach was far away now.

"Guys?" Her voice was so far away, so not her own. Tiffany and Derek wobbled into her vision. The earth beneath her butt shook and something crested the top of the hill, moved toward them. The street was a throat and a tongue unraveled, yellow and orange and red and moving and it was coming to get them.

It was coming to take them somewhere.

It was a whale it was a jellyfish it floated it swam it sank. Hundreds and thousands of fireflies flew into her ears, they flew into her eyes, and they sang and chattered and it was a bus.

It was a school bus.

It pulled up in front of them, and it was huge and it didn't look like the school bus usually looked and how strange to be going on a field trip this time of night. Pale faces loomed out and stared at her and they were late and they were going somewhere exciting and they better get on before they missed it.

The door unhinged like a jaw and the stairs were teeth and their buzzing friends ushered them on and she and Tiffany and Derek floated up and on and they sat down and they were surrounded by their classmates and no one was speaking and that was fine. It wasn't going to be a long trip. She knew that. Not much longer now.

She would sleep for a little while before they got there because everything was soft and warm and the lights flashed behind her eyelids but they were soft now and she drifted.

The bus moved like lapping waves. Fluttering motions pressed around her, tickled her lips, her eyelids. She smiled, couldn't help it, and legs caressed her throat, let loose a sticky substance and her throat stuck together but she didn't choke, she was fine, she was okay. Finally.

Tendrils of velvety flesh stroked her thighs, murmured questions, slid into her skull. They almost had it all. She could feel that there wasn't much left to give, but they wanted her to relax, and she wanted to relax, something stressful had happened lately, and it felt good to be in the arms of someone who loved her.

And they did love her. They loved every inch of her. Cheeks flushed with heat, nipples throbbed erect as wings buzzed against them, brushed against them so delicately, making them harder than she could bear, sweet cold gummy suction that made her shiver and they were dancing between her legs, they were crawling through her stomach, through the viscera there, cataloguing and reorganizing and it should hurt but it didn't. It felt sweet.

They held her heart, wrapped it in slithering black tongues, and her closed eyelids bled red red red, and the pressure on her heart made her gasp and the pressure between her legs made her writhe, and something slid into her cunt all the way, so thin and hard and it squirmed its way up, made new holes, found its way through her ribs into her brain and tickled all the pleasure centers there and she came and she didn't come and she came and everything was going to be fine.

# CHAPTER 19

**T**IME BENDED AND melted and they traveled and her friends were close far close and she was floating floating so relaxed so tired so safe.

The bus stopped. Flashing red light screamed her awake. No time for panic to set in, wet liquid buzzing flooded through her body, kept her calm, kept her safe.

The walls of the bus trembled, meaty, warm. The seat beneath her pushed, helped her up, and hands, soft soft hands moved her forward.

It was time to go.

It had been a long time since she had been on a field trip. It would be wonderful. There was so much to learn. Her classmates were talking again and she couldn't quite make out what they were saying. Their faces stayed still and their mouths didn't move, but they were excited, she could feel it. The sky bulged with bright red light and she could smell the ocean. Tiffany sat behind her, and a smile was visible on her face, barely, under all that . . . all that . . .

Derek was on the other side of the aisle and something was wrapped around his hand and he was gasping a little and the front of his pants were wet but he smiled at her and they were all fine. They were all fine. Huge flashing faces stared at her, tendrils waved and weaved and caressed at her face, her thighs, her nipples, and was she naked again? Strange to be naked on a field trip but she didn't feel like she would get in trouble and Tiffany was naked too, the stuff was all over her arms where she had held Sarah and her face where she had buried her head in Sarah's hair and her chest and everything, everything where she had touched her.

Derek's hand didn't look right but there was nothing to worry about everything was fine.

The doors swung open and the tendrils pushed her forward like waves, like the ocean waves and she laughed because that made sense, because they were at the ocean, and wasn't that funny?

Wasn't it?

They were on a field trip and it was to a place she had been before, a place she knew very well. Sarah stepped off the bus and the sand was so soft she fell and it hurt, she fell on her stomach and her stomach hurt and sand got in the wound and oh shit oh shit oh shit.

The sky was looking down at her and the way its eyes flashed made her feel insane. The things surrounded her, completely, and everything was red but it was so so dark too, it was the darkest night ever and she couldn't see Tiffany or Derek anymore, the beach was full of the creatures, and they were all speaking at once, so excited, and now her stomach was starting to hurt again, the things were moving again and she felt awake, she felt too fucking awake and the things were all around her and they were *hungry*.

"Tiffany!" She screamed. "Tiffany, where are you?"

# THE WRITHING SKIES

Tiffany said something, nearby or far away, Sarah couldn't tell, and then everything fell away except red and pain and hungry mouths opened so fucking wide and her stomach bulged, the flashing lights were inside her, snakes tented out of her skin, swirled beneath the fat, burrowed into muscle, and she couldn't breathe it hurt so much it hurt so fucking much.

*I'm not okay I'm not okay I'm not okay.*

Everything burst at once, all the swollen sores ripped apart in a splatter of hot luminescent fluid. Torrents of liquid splattered the sand, turned it to phosphorescent muck, and she was choking and screaming and fluid streamed from her mouth, her ears, her cunt. The excited murmur never let up, pried at her ears, and fat pale worms writhed out of her gut, out of her agony, between layers of skin they ripped their way through, leaving empty gaping holes and torn membrane and the sand and the screaming and the worms were beautiful.

So beautiful.

They were glowing angels that slithered through the sky, her skin and fat and tendon hung off them in clumps, they sang and floated and the glowing figures rushed forward, plucked them from the air and shoved them into mouths black with rot and they chewed and gnashed and sighed and Sarah closed her eyes and pressed her hands to her stomach, felt holes chewed through her skin, felt where she was empty.

*Rrr? Rrr? Rrr?* Still more questions, always more questions, and what fucking more did she have to give?

*Rrr? Rrr? Rrr?*

Everyone was talking at once.

A gnashing of teeth, a screaming, a warning.

The sky was speaking.

Hands and soft fingers and buzzing fireflies and she swatted them away, but there were so many of them, they lifted her, gently, touching, reaching inside her holes. They buoyed her up, and she floated through the mud, left her stinking mess behind. They ushered her forward.

The ocean was churning black blood and they had so many questions for her and she couldn't answer any of them. Their tendrils were in her eyes and her ears and her nose and in every orifice and it didn't feel good anymore and she didn't know what they wanted.

The air was cloudy and hard to breathe and little star creatures floated by, blinking. *Fireflies.*

The sky rumbled and it was so hungry. The mouth was opening, tearing apart the sky, a jagged rip that made her feel insane, all those teeth, all those teeth.

Everything was wet, her hair, her face, her eyes. Stinging salt flushed Sarah's gaping stomach.

She was in the water.

They were walking through the ocean and the ocean didn't exist. They were walking through their minds and in the distance the sky was chewing up the horizon and it was hungry for more, it was hungry to know more.

"Sarah!"

The crowds were thinning out now. Where were they going? There were still so many of them, they were still everywhere, but there was more space between them now, so much space. There was space between every grain of sand but there was Tiffany, finally, and up ahead, Derek, and ahead of that, in the water, a huge slab of goop like a jellyfish, a phosphorescent globe that thrust out of the water, glowing and beautiful.

Sarah grabbed on to Tiffany and Tiffany moaned and Sarah's hands sank into the ruined flesh on her arm and Tiffany screamed and Sarah whispered, "I'm sorry I'm sorry I'm sorry," but whether it was for what was happening to Tiffany's body, or her own, or for all of this, she didn't know.

They were pushed ahead into the freezing water that didn't feel like water, didn't feel like anything. They were all crying, couldn't stop. It didn't matter. The creatures were slow but steady, shoved them gently into the globe. It was sticky and shining and there was no choice but to crawl. Incandescent lights glowed from within. Sarah's feet sank into the strange flesh. It wobbled. Deep within the blob, shapes moved, and the ocean was gone, all that lay beneath them was space, more stars, more eyes, more mouths, until she couldn't look anymore, until she was too dizzy and Tiffany took her hand and they crawled up to the top.

The surface was smooth and she wouldn't look down because she could see too far. She could see too much.

A slab of *something* pushed out of the jelly-flesh. It was hard-edged and solid, and the place it burst from looked painful, swollen. Bruised blisters surrounded its base, leaking glowing fluid. The rectangular slab looked like meat, like the side of a cow, red and dripping, smears of fat and veins. An odor like spoiled food permeated the air.

"The fuck *is* that?" Derek's voice cracked, and at the sound of it, the sky moved closer, dribbled like ink, became a vast blanket above them that threatened to drop at any moment. All the eyes were looking at them, spinning wildly in their sockets, and the huge vicious mouth was grinning. Membranes of drool dripped down, hit Sarah on the shoulders, slugs that licked her skin and tasted her and asked more questions, always more questions.

The crowd surrounded them and pushed them and murmured and Sarah and Tiffany and Derek stumbled and the eyes peered down at them and the mouth opened wider. Holes ripped above them, the sky stretched and tore, and *the holes were in her skin and the holes were in the sky and the holes were the same* and it inched closer, flashed impossible colors. A poisonous tongue snaked out, ready to taste them, ready to finally bring this whole fucking mess to an end.

*Rrrrrr? Rrrr?*

The slab of flesh woke up with a scream, pulsed red hot, flashing in time with the eyes. The pushing stopped, the voices stopped and everything ground to a halt except the hunger.

"We need to feed it." Derek's voice didn't sound like his own. "It's so hungry. Can you feel it? Can't you feel how hungry it is?" His eyes were wet. The rotting flesh from his arm dripped onto the membrane below them and sizzled.

In the distance, there was nothing. The sky was too close, the sky was insane, the sky was inches away from their faces and it was *waiting*. Sarah took Tiffany's hand. The scenery was all chewed up, rotten, wrong. The flopping creatures pressed against them from all angles. The holes shone with a thin phosphorescence. No escape.

*Rrr? Rrrr? Rrrr?* Small noises. Getting inpatient

now. The figures flopped and gestured and tiny bits of them flaked away, into the waiting mouth. Red eyes spun and everything was too close and too claustrophobic and Sarah couldn't think.

"Who is it gonna be, you guys? It's . . . it's not gonna be me." He gestured with his arm, "This looks gross, but I'm practically fine. I can still be normal. Sarah!" He stumbled towards her, but tripped on the goop beneath his feet. "Sarah, we can still be normal. Those things are out of you. We can get out of here. We just have to feed it."

Tiffany's face hardened under the rot. She was absolutely covered in it. It looked painful, so painful. The tears that leaked from her eyes wove trails in the diseased flesh.

"Where the fuck are we gonna go from here, Derek? There's nothing." Sarah gestured, useless.

"No. There's something. We can be okay. Some of us. Maybe if we feed it, it'll let us go. Maybe . . . " The stubble stood out on his cheeks. His arm hung by his side. His body had been the least affected. Just his arm. His face still looked the same, sad and desperate. His features weren't handsome, not exactly, but she had grown to love them.

Tiffany hung back as Sarah helped him up.

The noises got louder. The red light was getting deeper, and it made new crevices in Tiffany's skin. The substance tightened and hardened and she groaned.

"She's not well, Sarah. She knows—you know, don't you Tiffany? It's gotta be you. It's fair. It's fair. Sarah and me, we can be okay."

Sarah's ruined stomach said otherwise. The wounds tunneled deep inside. How deep did they go? She shouldn't even be standing.

She felt so empty now.

In those holes, she could see the sky.

In the sky, the eyes leered, and the mouth was *hungry,* and the holes gaped open, drooling membranes obscured her vision but behind them, she could see light and shapes and something, something else. Was it her imagination, or was that the beach? Was that the sand and the sky and the normal world and was Derek right? Was there a way out of this? Was there a way back?

"We gotta do something. I can't wait on you forever."

"Fuck you." Tiffany's voice was muffled, and a stream of pus escaped her mouth when she spoke.

The sky ground its teeth and screamed, and the scream rumbled deep into Sarah's body, echoing in her new holes, the fireflies surrounding them screamed in response and everything was screaming and Derek was moving towards Tiffany. Sarah took his hand.

His bad hand.

She took his bad hand and yanked, and tiny jellyfish swam out of it and streams of black gunk spurted and the sky was laughing and now Derek was screaming and Sarah jammed her fingers into the gunk and ripped and he stumbled and she shoved.

And he was on the slab.

The tongue was deep and dark and redder than blood, glowing red, redder than anything she had ever seen, hundreds and thousands of gaping mouths opened within it with teeth, more teeth, tiny sharp razor teeth, and the tongue leaped out and wrapped around Derek's waist and it *sliced* and she could see his insides and he couldn't scream he didn't have time to scream and slime dripped and covered his face and sizzled and then he was in the teeth, and razor sharpness tore into his tender flesh, and scraps of flesh dripped down and the creatures on the ground reached and fought and tasted and Derek had no last words. He was just fucking gone.

And was that finally fucking enough?

Her stomach moved. Bits of her drifted to the ground. Tiffany grabbed Sarah's shoulder. She couldn't see any of her features anymore, just one eye, but that one eye was better than Sarah's because Sarah couldn't breathe and couldn't think but Tiffany could, Tiffany pointed, and one of the holes in the sky was so close, was inches away, and it looked like the beach. It looked like the normal beach with normal colors and the questions were starting again *rrr? rrr? rrr?* and there was no time. No time.

So they leaped into the sky.

# CHAPTER 20

**THERE WAS A** moment when Sarah thought she would tangle in membranes like a spider web and be stuck there forever, but they broke through with a gentle pop. They fell into the sand.

"Oh . . . Oh. Oh." Tears were a relief, leaked tension from her head. The sky was blue and full of clouds and normal. The ocean was salty sweet and the water lapped, fresh against her aching feet. The sun was in the sky.

"Oh god." Tiffany blubbered, and Sarah turned and she could see her face, and it was the most beautiful thing she had ever seen, she could see her eyes and her mouth and her nose. Laughter and tears and everything was okay.

*I'm okay I'm okay I'm okay.*

"Oh my god, it's over. Is it over? It's over?" The sand was soft, too soft to walk in, and they pulled each other up. The sun was in the sky and surely that was the sun and their car must be nearby and everything was how it was supposed to be, except Derek was gone, and good fucking riddance.

"Thank god. Thank god." Sarah stumbled in the sand, fell, laughed, she couldn't stop laughing. She rolled over and looked up at the sky and it had never felt so good to look at the sky and see only clouds.

They must be clouds.

Tiffany stood over her, smiling, and that blue tinge to her skin, it was only the lighting. It was only the time of day. That shine, it was just happiness. There was nothing moving there. There couldn't be. It was over. Those lights weren't lights, the sky was blue, the sky was just normal fucking blue.

Sarah closed her eyes.

She reached beneath the sweatshirt, her hand trailed from thigh to smooth flat tummy, and her fingers sank into a tunnel, came out sticky.

Tiffany said something, but Sarah couldn't hear her.

*Rrr?*

*Rrr?*

Her fingers tingled, dripped, and even with her closed eyes she could see the colors flashing.

# ABOUT THE AUTHOR

Betty Rocksteady is made of 1920's Max Fleischer cartoons, cats and a smattering of digusting goop. This is her third novella, and probably the grossest. Find out more about her art and fiction at www.bettyrocksteady.com.

**Potential Triggers: General horror themes, body horror, general themes of sexual violence, emotionally abusive relationship, date rape, rape by nonhuman entity, violent miscarriage scene.**

Potential triggers including sexual manipulation by alien entities may be in any chapter, but the most explicit chapters are detailed below:

CHAPTER 3: Sarah crawls into the bushes to hide from the cloaked figures. She is raped by unseen tentacles that are able to manipulate her body into enjoying it. They leave something in her stomach tissue. Shocked and horrified, she crawls away.

CHAPTER 7: Derek physically pressures Sarah to have sex. She has a flashback to when he raped her without a condom. In the present time, Derek slips his hand into her shirt but is horrified to find the alien substance that coats her abdomen. He storms away toward the school, angry.

CHAPTER 15: A flashback to Derek, Tiffany and Sarah on a beach. Derek attempts to give Sarah an abortion by punching and stomping on her stomach while Tiffany holds her. The violence and emotional turmoil attract the attention of an alien entity in the sky. Phosphorescent creatures rain down and the sky swallows them.

IF YOU ENJOYED *THE WRITHING SKIES*, DON'T PASS UP ON THESE OTHER TITLES FROM PERPETUAL MOTION MACHINE . . .

# LIKE JAGGED TEETH
## BY BETTY ROCKSTEADY

ISBN: 978-1-943720-21-7
Page count: 118
$11.95

The guys following her home are bad enough, but when Jacalyn's Poppa comes to the rescue, things only get worse. After all, he's been dead for six years. There's no time to be relieved, because when she ends up back at Poppa's new apartment, nothing feels right. The food here doesn't taste how food should taste. The doors don't work how doors are supposed to work. And something's not right with Poppa. Guilt and sickness spiral Jacalyn into a nightmarish new reality of Lynchian hallucinations and grotesque body horror.

# THE GREEN KANGAROOS
## BY JESSICA MCHUGH

ISBN: 978-0-9860594-6-9
Page count: 184
$12.95

Perry Samson loves drugs. He'll take what he can get, but raw atlys is his passion. Shot hard and fast into his testicles, atlys helps him forget that he lives in an abandoned Baltimore school, that his roommate exchanges lumps of flesh for drugs at the Kum Den Smokehouse, and that every day is a moldering motley of whores, cuntcutters, and disease. Unfortunately, atlys never helps Perry forget that, even though his older brother died from an atlys overdose, he will never stop being the tortured middle child.

Set in 2099, THE GREEN KANGAROOS explores the disgusting world of Perry's addiction to atlys and the Samson family's addiction to his sobriety.

# THE DETAINED
## BY KRISTOPHER TRIANA

ISBN: 978-1-943720-26-2

Page count: 112

$12.95

When Phoebe McBride returns to Bonneville for her twentieth high school reunion, she tells herself it's the best way to confront what has haunted her since her senior year. There was one boy who never lived to see graduation, and in a way she blames herself for this tragedy. Now a child psychologist, Phoebe is determined to face her demons by going back, but those demons may be fresher than she realizes.

When she arrives at the school there are only three of her old classmates present—a bad boy turned writer, a fallen football hero and a popular girl whose life isn't all she'd thought it would be. Bonneville isn't even set up for a party—it's set up for detention. Tables are aligned and her old P.E. teacher sits waiting. He always hosted detention back in her school days, but now he thinks he's here to accept an award for all his years of service.

Soon the guests discover gruesome keepsakes waiting on their chairs. Horror and paranoia sink their claws into the class of '96 as they are forced to revisit the worst memory from their youth, and ultimately pay for their past.

# The Perpetual Motion Machine Catalog

*Baby Powder and Other Terrifying Substances* |
John C. Foster | Story Collection

*Bleed* | Various Authors | Anthology

*Bone Saw* | Patrick Lacey | Novel

*Crabtown, USA:Essays & Observations* |
Rafael Alvarez | Essays

*Dead Men* | John Foster | Novel

*Destroying the Tangible Issue of Reality; or, Searching
for Andy Kaufmann* | T. Fox Dunham | Novel

*The Detained* | Kristopher Triana | Novella

*Gods on the Lam* | Christopher David Rosales | Novel

*Gory Hole* | Craig Wallwork | Story Collection

*The Green Kangaroos* | Jessica McHugh | Novel

*Invasion of the Weirdos* | Andrew Hilbert | Novel

*Last Dance in Phoenix* | Kurt Reichenbaugh | Novel

*Like Jagged Teeth* | Betty Rocksteady | Novella

*Live On No Evil* | Jeremiah Israel | Novel

*Long Distance Drunks: a Tribute to Charles
Bukowski* | Various Authors | Anthology

*Lost Films* | Various Authors | Anthology

*Lost Signals* | Various Authors | Anthology

*Mojo Rising* | Bob Pastorella | Novella

*Night Roads* | John Foster | Novel

*Quizzleboon* | John Oliver Hodges | Novel

*The Perpetual Motion Club* | Sue Lange | Novel

*The Ritalin Orgy* | Matthew Dexter | Novel

*The Ruin Season* | Kristopher Triana | Novel

*So it Goes: a Tribute to Kurt Vonnegut* | Various Authors | Anthology

*Speculations* | Joe McKinney | Story Collection

*Tales from the Holy Land* | Rafael Alvarez | Story Collection

*The Nightly Disease* | Max Booth III | Novel

*The Tears of Isis* | James Dorr | Story Collection

*The Train Derails in Boston* | Jessica McHugh | Novel

*The Violators* | Vincenzo Bilof | Novel

*Time Eaters* | Jay Wilburn | Novel

*Vampire Strippers from Saturn* | Vincenzo Bilof | Novel

**Patreon:**
www.patreon.com/pmmpublishing

**Website:**
www.PerpetualPublishing.com

**Facebook:**
www.facebook.com/PerpetualPublishing

**Twitter:**
@PMMPublishing

**Newsletter:**
www.PMMPNews.com

**Email Us:**
Contact@PerpetualPublishing.com